sheil

'I want to see

'I've missed the f[...]
think I have the ri[...]

'All right. But I want you to understand that Hannah doesn't know anything about you. Claire...well, Claire decided that it was better not to tell her in the circumstances.'

'And you agreed to keep the secret, didn't you?' He smiled thinly. 'You and Claire erased me from Hannah's life—but the situation is going to change from here on, believe me.'

'What do you mean?'

'That I intend to make up for all those lost years. Hannah needs a father. She needs me in more ways than you ever realised!'

He had a right to be angry, a right even to blame her for keeping her promise to Claire, but did he have the right to disrupt Hannah's life? Could she really trust him not to break her precious niece's heart?

Could she trust him not to break her own heart as well?

Jennifer Taylor lives in the north-west of England with her husband Bill and children Mark and Vicky. She had been writing Mills & Boon® romances for some years, but when she discovered Medical Romances™ she was so captivated by these heart-warming stories that she set out to write them herself! When not writing or doing research for her latest book, Jennifer's hobbies include reading, travel, walking her dog and retail therapy (shopping!). Jennifer claims all that bending and stretching to reach the shelves is the best exercise possible.

A CHESHIRE PRACTICE
Where love is just a heartbeat away.

A wonderful new series of stories
set in the Winton Surgery—a GP practice in the heart
of Cheshire. Follow the drama of a country practice
and the lives and loves of the people who work there
in these delightful books from Jennifer Taylor.

**Look out for the second story
set in the Winton Surgery—coming soon.**

ADAM'S
DAUGHTER

BY
JENNIFER TAYLOR

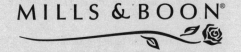

First published in Great Britain 2001
Harlequin Mills & Boon Limited,
Eton House, 18-24 Paradise Road, Richmond, Surrey TW9 1SR

© Jennifer Taylor 2001

ISBN 0 263 82686 4

Set in Times Roman 10¼ on 11¼ pt.
03-0901-57625

Printed and bound in Spain
by Litografía Rosés, S.A., Barcelona

CHAPTER ONE

ELIZABETH CAMPBELL was about to break the most solemn vow she had ever made. It was little wonder that her hands were shaking as she reached for the telephone. Seven years ago she had promised her sister, Claire, that she would never try to contact Adam Knight under any circumstances. Even though she'd had misgivings about the decision Claire had made, Beth had kept her word.

Until now.

Her deep green eyes were shadowed as she dialled the number. It had taken her some time to track him down. At one point she had feared that she would never find him and then late last night, as she had been going through some of Claire's old diaries, she had found his phone number. She knew that the likelihood of her being able to reach him on it after all these years was very slim, but it was the only lead she had.

The problem was that Claire had told her very little about Adam Knight. All Beth knew was that her sister had met him at a hospital in London where she had been doing her pre-registration training.

Claire had been typically honest about their relationship. She hadn't tried to pretend that Adam had been the love of her life. They'd had a brief affair then they'd gone their separate ways. When Claire had written to him a few months later he hadn't replied, so it was hardly surprising that Beth found herself beset by doubts once again when she heard the phone ringing.

Even if she did manage to contact Adam Knight, what right did she have to ask him for help? Surely he had made it clear all those years ago that he wasn't interested?

'Yes?'

The voice that answered was deep, male and heavily laced with impatience. It only served to make Beth feel even more nervous so that she found herself stammering. 'I—I'd like to s-speak to Adam Knight if he's available, please.'

'Speaking. However, I was just on my way out and I don't have the time to hang about. I can give you thirty seconds and that's it.'

'Oh, I see. Maybe I should phone back later,' she began, stunned that she had found him at last. She certainly didn't want to make a mess of things by blurting out the reason why she was phoning.

'That sounds like a good idea,' he said, briskly interrupting her. 'If I'm not in then leave your number on the machine and I'll get back to you at some point. OK?'

He hung up before she could reply. Beth slowly replaced the receiver then took a deep breath. Hardly the most auspicious of starts! If that was an indication of Adam Knight's character then she might have to rethink her plans. He hadn't sounded like the kind of man who would put himself out for anyone, but she'd already suspected that.

It was a worrying thought but she tried not to dwell on it as she got ready for work. She had been working at Winton Surgery for almost a month now and she loved her new job. She had been desperate to leave St Jude's so she'd applied for the post of practice nurse at the busy Cheshire surgery as soon as she'd seen the advertisement. The fact that a self-contained flat over the surgery had come with the job had been an added bonus.

The price of accommodation in the town was horrendous and she doubted whether she would have been able to afford more than a bedsit on her salary. Now, as she finished pinning up her shoulder-length, red-gold hair and looked around the sunlit bedroom, she gave a little sigh of relief. At least she had somewhere decent for them to live when Hannah came home...

If Hannah came home, a small voice reminded her chillingly.

Beth's eyes were sad as she picked up the photograph of her niece from the bedside table. The picture had been taken the previous year and Hannah looked so happy in it. She had been wearing a new dress at the time—bright blue cotton with big yellow daisies printed all over it—and she had looked so adorable with her mass of black curls and sparkling blue eyes.

It was hard to look at the photograph and realise how different the child looked now, but it helped to firm Beth's resolve. She *had* been right to contact Adam Knight. She would phone him again as soon as she finished work, only this time she would make sure that he found the time to listen to what she had to say!

Beth left the flat and went down to the surgery. It was barely eight but she wasn't surprised when she found Christopher Andrews, the junior partner, already at his desk. There had been a bit of a crisis the previous week when the senior partner, Jonathan Wright, had been rushed into hospital for emergency heart bypass surgery. Nobody had suspected that Jonathan had been ill because he had always seemed so full of life.

Beth had grown to admire the older doctor in the few weeks she had been working at the surgery, and had been saddened when he had been taken ill. Now she tapped on Chris's door to see if he had any news about how Jonathan was faring.

'What's the latest on Jonathan?' she asked when Chris beckoned her into the room. Chris was in his late thirties, unmarried and, according to Eileen Marshall, their receptionist, totally dedicated to his job. However, she couldn't help noticing how tired he looked that day.

'As well as can be expected was what I was told this morning when I phoned the hospital.' Chris sighed as he tossed his spectacles onto the desk and rubbed his eyes. 'Which could mean anything, couldn't it?'

'Hospital-speak for mind your own business,' Beth teased. 'I have to confess to using that very same phrase myself when I was on the coronary care unit.'

'I'd forgotten that you worked there,' Chris said, frowning. 'It feels as though you've been here for ever, to be honest. You've fitted in so well that I can't believe that you've worked here for only a few weeks.'

'Coming up to a month now,' she said, smiling at the compliment. 'I'm almost a fully fledged member of the Winton team. Just two more weeks to go and hopefully I should get my wings!'

'I think you can forget about being here on a trial basis. Jonathan was saying last week how pleased he is with your work.' Chris sighed again. 'I only hope that I won't let him down. It's going to be tough keeping on top of this job, especially when Jonathan is such a hard act to follow.'

'Surely you're going to need help?' Beth said, frowning at the thought of Chris trying to cope on his own. The surgery was extremely busy and she couldn't imagine him keeping up with all the work by himself.

'I certainly am. I'm not Superman and I don't mind admitting it! Fortunately, I believe reinforcements are on the way. When I last spoke to Mary, she told me that she had contacted her nephew and that he was flying home. Evidently, he has offered to cover until Jonathan is better.'

'I didn't know Jonathan and Mary had a nephew who's a doctor,' Beth exclaimed.

'It's been a while since he's been back to England,' Chris explained. 'He's been working for the WHO in Rwanda and before that he was in India, I believe. I met him only briefly when I first came here but we got on extremely well. He's a nice chap, takes after Jonathan in that he's totally committed to his work.'

'He'd have to be if he's been doing aid work on a long-term basis,' she observed. 'It takes a certain type of person to cope with that kind of work.'

'It certainly does. It will be a big change for him, working here, but I'm delighted to know that I won't be on my own for very much longer. It's busy enough here even when we're fully staffed!'

The words turned out to be prophetic because it was one of the busiest mornings Beth could recall since she had started at the surgery. Although she had enjoyed her job at St Jude's, the sheer diversity of the work she did at the surgery meant that there was always something new to deal with each day, and that day was no exception.

She smiled to herself as she finished cleaning a particularly bad graze on a four-year-old's knee. So far that morning she'd supervised a teenager who was learning to inject himself with insulin, treated a nasty ulcer on an octogenarian's leg and taken copious amounts of blood for various tests. There was never a dull moment in general practice, it seemed!

'Now, can you be a really brave boy and sit on the couch while I check that there's no more gravel in your knee?' she asked, smiling at little Michael Thomas, who had been brought into the surgery by his anxious grandmother after tripping over in the park.

Michael stared solemnly at her, tears still sparkling on his thick blond lashes. He'd been sobbing his heart out when he'd been brought into Beth's room but he'd quietened down under her gentle ministrations. He gave a hesitant nod and she smiled reassuringly as she lifted him onto the couch.

'What a brave boy you are!' She turned to Mrs Thomas, his grandmother. 'I think I've got all the gravel out but I just want to make certain before I put a dressing on Michael's knee.'

'That's why I thought I should bring him here,' the older lady explained. 'My eyes aren't as good as they used to be and I was afraid that I might not see all the little bits of dirt.

It's such a nasty cut, isn't it? I only took my eyes off him for a second, too.'

'You can't watch a child all the time,' Beth consoled her. 'At this age they are always getting into mischief.' She took a big magnifying glass from a drawer and showed it to Michael. 'I'm going to use this to look through. It will help me see if there's any more dirt in that cut.'

She held up the magnifying glass so that he could see through it and smiled when he chuckled at the distorted image of her face. He seemed more fascinated than afraid when she carefully examined his knee with the help of the glass.

'Me see, me see!' he demanded, leaning forward and threatening to topple off the couch in his eagerness to have a look.

Beth quickly steadied him then held the magnifying glass so that he could get a good view of the cut. 'Can you see any more gravel in it, Michael?' she asked, and he shook his head importantly.

'No. All gone.'

'Good. That's what I wanted to hear. Now, sit back while I put a dressing over that poor knee. I'm sure Granny doesn't want to have to take you home with a sore knee *and* a sore head if you fall off the couch.'

Mrs Thomas laughed. 'I certainly don't! My daughter-in-law won't trust me to take him out again if I return him home looking like one of the walking wounded!' She lowered her voice conspiratorially. 'Actually, I think Diane was trying to get me out of the way and that's why she suggested I take Michael to the park. It's my seventieth birthday soon and I think Diane and Robert, my son, are planning a surprise for me.'

'We're having a party, Granny,' Michael piped up. 'Only Mummy said that it's a secret.'

Beth laughed. 'Not any longer it isn't!'

Now that she was sure that the cut was clean, she covered

it with some antiseptic-impregnated gauze then added a large adhesive dressing printed with cartoon characters.

Michael was entranced by the dressing. Beth chuckled as she followed him out to Reception and watched him leaving the surgery, bent almost double so that he could look at his knee.

'One more satisfied customer, wouldn't you agree?' she said to Eileen behind the desk.

'I certainly would. If only they were all so easy to please… Well, look who's here! Where did you spring from, stranger?'

Beth looked round to see who the receptionist was speaking to and felt a frisson run down her spine when she saw the tall, dark haired man who had just entered the surgery. He was handsome enough to have warranted a second or even a third look but it wasn't that which kept her staring at him. There was just something strangely familiar about him, yet she knew for a fact that they had never met.

'I arrived late last night—very late, in fact!' He gave a deep chuckle as the middle-aged receptionist rushed round the desk and gave him a hug. 'But it was worth it to be on the receiving end of a greeting like that! It's good to see you Eileen. You're looking great.'

Beth felt another ripple run through her. Not only did he *look* familiar, he sounded familiar, too! But where on earth had she heard that voice before?

She reran the mellifluous tones through her head but she couldn't place them. She was still trying to pin down the elusive memory when the man turned towards her and Beth saw a frown cross his handsome face.

'I know this must sound crazy but have we met?' He stared at her then shrugged. 'You look so familiar but I can't for the life of me recall where I've seen you before.'

'You'll have to do better than that!' Eileen laughed as she linked her arm through his and led him to the desk. 'You don't honestly think that Beth is going to fall for that old line? It's got whiskers on it!'

'I'm out of practice. That's my excuse and I'm sticking to it!'

He chuckled softly as he reached Beth, his dark blue eyes crinkling at the corners as he smiled at her. Now that he was standing in front of her she could tell that he must be at least six feet tall, with broad shoulders and a powerful chest tapering down to slim hips and incredibly long legs. He was casually dressed in khaki chinos and a matching shirt, and although the clothes were clean they were very creased.

Beth had a strong impression of a man to whom material possessions meant very little. Everything he was wearing was functional but basic, from his clothes to the inexpensive watch strapped to his broad wrist by means of a plain leather band. Whoever he was, he certainly didn't feel the need to impress people by his appearance, she decided, surprised by the speed with which she had made such a judgement.

'OK, then, I'll try again—but this is for Eileen's benefit, mind you. I know better than to fall out with the one woman around here who knows how to make a decent cup of coffee.' He held out his hand and for some reason Beth found herself obediently taking it.

'Of all the surgeries in all the towns in all the world, I have to run into you here.' He grinned engagingly at her. 'Now, if you could just tell me who you are and put me out of my misery I shall be eternally grateful. If we have met before then I apologise for not remembering where and when. Jet lag does tend to liquidise the brain cells, I'm afraid.'

'I don't believe that we have met,' she replied, laughing at his rueful expression. 'Although I have to confess that I had a feeling that I'd seen you somewhere before when you walked in.'

'Maybe we met in another life,' he suggested lightly.

However, she wasn't blind to the frown which had crossed his face while she'd been speaking.

The telephone rang and Eileen regretfully excused herself to answer it. It was obvious that the receptionist was intrigued by what was happening but Beth decided that it might be better to call a halt. She had work to do and that had to come first, pleasant though this interlude had been.

'Who knows?' she replied with a smile as she started to withdraw her hand. However, the stranger held onto it.

'You still haven't told me who you are.'

'So I haven't. Sorry. I'm Beth Campbell, the new practice nurse—' She stopped when she heard his swift intake of breath, feeling her heart start to race when she felt his fingers tighten around hers.

'You're Claire's sister, aren't you? No wonder you seemed so familiar when I first saw you. You look a lot like her.' The blue eyes swept over her before coming back to her face, and she saw the regret they held. 'I was so sorry when I heard that she had been killed. I was out of the country at the time and I didn't find out what had happened until months later. It was a shock even though I hadn't seen her in years.'

'You knew Claire?' Beth whispered. She withdrew her hand abruptly, afraid that he would feel the tremors that were racing through her. Her mind was starting to fit together all the bits of the puzzle about who he was but she simply couldn't believe what it was telling her.

'Yes. We worked together in London, way back. We were good friends at one time, too. I'm Adam Knight, by the way. Maybe she mentioned me?'

'Yes, she did.' Beth could feel the ground tilting beneath her feet and knew that she had to get away before she disgraced herself. 'I'd better get back to work. I've still got patients to see.'

'And I'd better let Chris know that I'm here. I'd have been here earlier only I wanted to stop by the hospital to see how uncle Jonathan was doing,' he replied easily, but she could see the puzzlement in his eyes and knew that he had been surprised by her brusqueness.

'Dr Wright is your uncle?' she asked hollowly. That Adam Knight was not only here in Winton but actually about to start work at the surgery was too much to take in. She felt as though she had woken in the middle of some sort of crazy dream.

'Yes. Funnily enough, that's how Claire and I met. She overheard me saying that I had an uncle in Winton and told me that she had grown up not far from here.' Adam sighed. 'It's strange how these things happen. I'm not sure if you can call it coincidence or fate.'

Neither was she!

Beth murmured something, although she couldn't recall what she'd said a moment later. She hurried back to her room and closed the door, needing a few minutes to compose herself before calling in her next patient. But how easy was it going to be to deal with this situation?

Discovering that Adam Knight had links with the surgery changed everything. How could she risk asking him for help now when she had no idea how he might react? Maybe she was doing him an injustice, but she had always suspected that he must have known why Claire had wanted to see him, and that was why he hadn't replied to her letter.

He hadn't wanted to face up to his responsibilities, that was what it had boiled down to. In the circumstances, she'd known all along that asking him for help was a long shot. However, it was one thing to approach a stranger with the request but another entirely to broach it to a colleague. Frankly, the situation could become intolerable if he refused. This job was important to her and she didn't want to risk losing it…

More important to her than Hannah was? a small voice whispered.

She took a deep breath.

Nothing was more important than Hannah. Neither her job nor Adam Knight's feelings were of any consequence weighed against that. It was Hannah who mattered. Nobody else!

Somehow Beth got through the rest of her appointments with an outward show of calm which only she knew was a sham. She cleared up after her last patient had left then took the record cards through to the office for filing.

Eileen was getting ready to go home for lunch and she smiled cheerfully at her. 'Just leave them in the tray, dear, and I'll do them later. It didn't go too badly, all things considered, and now that Adam's back, we should cope until poor Dr Wright is better.'

Beth smiled and nodded in all the right places but she wasn't really listening. Her ears had picked up the sound of a surprisingly familiar voice. She had already prepared herself by the time Adam Knight and Chris Andrews appeared.

'I'm going to make a start on the house calls,' Chris informed them, poking his head round the door. 'Adam tells me that you two have introduced yourselves, Beth, so I don't need to go through the formalities. He's going to take this afternoon's antenatal clinic to save me having to race back. I might even get some lunch today so things must be looking up!'

He turned to the other man without waiting for her to answer. 'Thanks, Adam. It's great to have you here. I'll leave you in Beth's very capable hands.'

A small silence fell after Chris and Eileen left. Beth knew that Adam was still standing in the doorway but she couldn't bring herself to look at him. Should she tell him now why she had been trying to contact him or should she wait until later? They had to work together that afternoon and it could make the situation extremely difficult...

'Did Claire ever talk about me?'

She jumped when he spoke, feeling the colour rush to her

cheeks when she looked round and found him staring at her. 'Not really,' she replied, glad that she could be truthful because she doubted that she could have lied.

'Then she didn't say anything bad about me?' He must have seen her surprise because he smiled thinly. 'I got the distinct impression earlier that you were upset when you found out who I was. I just wondered if Claire might have said something.'

'Should she have done?' she countered.

'I've no idea.' He leant against the doorjamb and regarded her thoughtfully. 'We certainly didn't part on bad terms, not so far as I was concerned, anyway.'

'Then you have nothing to worry about, have you?' Beth gave him a tight little smile and went to the door, pausing when he made no attempt to get out of her way.

'How much did your sister tell you about our relationship?' he asked bluntly.

'Enough.' She met his gaze squarely, refusing to let him think that she was embarrassed in any way. 'Naturally, she didn't go into any detail but I know that you and Claire were lovers at one time, if that's what you mean.'

'I see. And how do you feel about the idea? Does it bother you?' he replied smoothly.

'No. How about you? Does it worry you that I know about you and Claire?' she shot back.

'Not at all.' He shrugged but his gaze was intent. 'It all happened a long time ago and it has little bearing on the present situation. There's no reason that I know of why my relationship with your sister should get in the way of us working together. However, I have a feeling that something is troubling you, despite what you've just said.'

Beth looked away because she simply couldn't stand there and meet that forceful stare any longer. Part of her wanted to tell him the truth and get it over with, whilst another part urged her to be cautious. Maybe it would be better to tread carefully until she had a better idea how he might react to her request.

'I was just surprised when you turned up here,' she said, choosing her words with care. 'Claire never told me much about you so I had no idea that you were related to Dr Wright.'

'I see. It must have been a shock for you, then,' he said quietly.

'It was.' He must have heard the ring of truth in her voice because he visibly relaxed. Beth felt a flurry race along her nerves when he suddenly smiled at her. She had noticed how attractive he was when they had first met but he was devastating when he smiled like that.

'And I'm not helping the situation by cross-examining you. Sorry. My excuse is that it was a surprise for me, too, to meet you here. Claire spoke about you many times. She was very fond of you, Beth.'

'I was very fond of her,' she admitted, feeling the ready tears welling into her eyes.

'Now I've upset you and that was the last thing I wanted to do.' His tone was so gentle that she had to swallow the lump that had formed in her throat before she could speak.

'It's not your fault. It's been a difficult year, what with Claire's death and…' She stopped as she realised what she had been about to say, feeling her heart racing when she saw the way Adam was looking at her again.

'And what? What were you going to say before you thought better of it?' he asked in a silky tone that made her shiver with apprehension. 'Why do I get the feeling that I'm missing something, Beth?'

'I…I don't know what you mean,' she murmured, avoiding his eyes.

'Don't you?' He paused, obviously giving her the chance to explain, but she knew that she wasn't ready to do that just yet. It was too important that she didn't make any mistakes. So much hinged on him agreeing…

Did she really think that he would agree, though? Everything she knew about him pointed to the fact that he might very well refuse. After all he hadn't bothered to answer Claire's letter, neither had he made any attempt to contact her in the last seven years. Were those the actions of a man who would be prepared to help?

She bit her lip in a quandary of indecision and heard him sigh. 'I'm doing it again, aren't I? Interrogating you?'

He smiled apologetically when she glanced at him but she could tell that he was still curious about the way she had been behaving, and was merely trying to smooth over an awkward moment.

'It's a rather strange situation for both of us,' she suggested diffidently.

'I suppose it is.' He frowned as though he was considering that idea. 'Neither of us could have imagined this happening in our wildest dreams.'

Amen to that! she silently endorsed then realised that he had carried on speaking.

'My problems?' she queried, her heart turning over as she wondered what he had meant by that. Had she been right all along? *Had* he guessed what Claire had wanted to tell him seven years ago? The thought suddenly made her feel sick, even though she had no idea why it should matter so much.

'Having to work with a doctor about whom you know absolutely zilch. It's no wonder you're on edge. You're probably worried stiff in case I make a complete hash of things this afternoon.'

He glanced down at his crumpled clothes and grimaced. 'I admit that I don't look the part of a bona fide GP, but I swear that I have all the necessary certificates to prove it somewhere around!'

She laughed shakily, not sure why she felt so relieved that he wasn't about to confess to such unscrupulous behaviour.

'You don't have to prove anything to me. I'm willing to take your word for it that you're suitably qualified.'

'Thank you. I appreciate it.' He treated her to a smile and once again Beth felt her pulse skip a beat. It had been such a long time since she'd reacted like that to a man's smile that it confused her, and it was a moment before she realised what Adam had said.

'The airline lost your luggage?' she repeated.

'That's right. I couldn't get a direct flight back to the UK so I had to make a couple of stop-overs *en route*. Somewhere between Tangiers and Düsseldorf my cases went AWOL. Fortunately, I had a holdall with me containing a change of clothes so at least I was able to wear something clean to come here today.'

He gave a deep chuckle. 'Aunt Mary is going to hunt out some of the stuff I left with her the last time I was in England, but I'm not sure if it will do much more to improve my image. I have never been known for my sartorial elegance, shall we say.'

He paused when the phone on the reception desk suddenly rang. 'I expect you want to go for lunch so I'll get that. Anything I need to know before this afternoon?'

'No, it's all quite straightforward—routine antenatal check-ups with, hopefully, few problems,' she assured him.

'Fine. I'll see you later, then.'

Adam hurried away and a moment later Beth heard the rumble of his voice as he picked up the receiver. However, she didn't wait around. Apart from the fact that she didn't want to have to answer any more awkward questions, she didn't have the time to hang around if she wanted to see Hannah before she was due back at work.

She sighed sadly.

Everything came back to Hannah. She just hadn't realised how difficult it was going to be to tell Adam about her niece.

CHAPTER TWO

'RIGHT, Mrs Graham. If you could pop up onto the couch then I can see how junior is doing.'

Adam smiled at the young woman. 'This baby certainly isn't in a rush to make his appearance in the world. You're what…three days overdue now?'

'That's right, Doctor,' Elaine Graham replied as Beth helped her get comfortable.

Elaine had looked extremely tense when she'd arrived. However, Beth couldn't help noticing how much more relaxed she now appeared to be. It was obvious that Adam's easygoing manner had had a positive effect on Elaine, as it had had on all the other expectant mums they had seen that afternoon. Beth had to admit that she was impressed.

'I was hoping this one would be early, unlike his brothers,' Elaine explained. 'My youngest is having a birthday party the day after tomorrow and I was hoping that I'd have had the baby by then.'

'Well, there's still time,' Adam assured her, gently feeling the position the baby was lying in. 'The baby's head is engaged so in theory it should be all systems go very soon.'

'I wish you'd tell that to the baby,' Elaine retorted. 'I've had three children so far, and each time I've been told that the birth is imminent and nothing has happened!'

'We don't get it right *every* time, Mrs Graham!' he admitted ruefully. He finished his examination then helped her to sit up. 'I just want to take your blood pressure again. The reading seemed to be a little on the high side when Sister Campbell took it earlier.'

'Probably because I'd been rushing round,' Elaine admitted, offering her arm so that he could wrap the cuff of the sphygmomanometer around it. 'There's always something that needs doing when you've got three lively boys.'

'I'm sure there is.' Adam quickly inflated the cuff then paused while he took the new reading. 'I don't know how you mums cope with everything. It's no wonder that there don't seem to be enough hours in a day. But will you promise me that you'll try to rest more until the baby arrives? It will help to keep your blood pressure down and that's very important at this stage.'

'I'll try, Dr Knight,' Elaine agreed readily, so readily, in fact, that Beth had to hide her amazement. She knew that Dr Wright had tried—and failed!—to make Elaine see how important it was that she rested during the latter stages of her pregnancy. Obviously, Adam's charm had garnered better results than Dr Wright's kindly paternalism had done.

It was unsettling to realise it. The image she had built up over the years of Adam Knight just didn't gel with what she had seen that afternoon. He had been kind and caring towards the patients, deeply sympathetic to any problems they'd had. She simply couldn't reconcile the cold professional of her imagination with the warmly attentive man she had been working with. It struck her that she could easily grow to like him, only she wasn't sure that would be a good thing. There wasn't room to start worrying about his feelings when she had Hannah to consider.

The thought of her niece made her sigh and she saw Adam glance at her. She forced herself to concentrate as he saw Elaine Graham out, not wanting to give him an opening to start questioning her again. He'd made no mention of their earlier conversation but she'd noticed him watching her several times and knew that he hadn't forgotten what had happened. Until she'd decided how she intended to handle this situation it seemed safer to err on the side of caution.

Beth set about packing up the blood samples that needed to be sent to the lab for testing. There were no more patients to be seen so once everywhere was tidy she would be free until evening surgery. Adam had come back into the room and she looked at him in surprise when he started stripping the paper sheets off the couch.

'I'll do that in a minute. You don't need to bother.'

'It'll be quicker if we both do it.' He bundled the sheets into a ball and shoved them into a plastic refuse sack then picked up the spray bottle of disinfectant and began wiping down the work surfaces.

Beth was more than a little startled by his actions and it must have showed.

'Old habits die hard, I'm afraid. I'm so used to having to clear up after myself that I feel positively embarrassed by the idea of anyone else doing it for me.' He squirted some of the disinfectant onto the couch then began vigorously rubbing the leather. 'Just ignore me. With a bit of luck I'll have worked it out of my system in a week or two.'

'By that time I might have got used to you performing such lowly tasks,' she replied, trying to inject a little levity into her voice. However, the sight of him working away like that was having the strangest effect on her.

She swallowed hard as she watched the muscles in his arms flex each time he rubbed the cloth over the couch. He had rolled up the sleeves of his shirt so that she had a perfect view of his tanned forearms. When he reached across to the far side of the couch and his shirt suddenly parted company from the waistband of his trousers to reveal a couple of inches of muscular back, she had to bite her lip. Yet why should the sight of an inch or two of exposed flesh make her feel as though her insides had turned to mush? she wondered.

'What else needs doing? Ah, yes. Those files need to go to the office.' He stowed the cloth away in the cupboard under the sink and turned. His eyes narrowed when he saw the guilty start she gave. 'Is something wrong?'

'No, of course not!' She gave a tinkly laugh, which

wouldn't have convinced anyone that she was telling the truth, and hurried on. 'Are you here for evening surgery?'

'I offered to split the list with Chris but he said that he could manage. I think he was worried that I might keel over from jet lag,' he explained, although she could tell that she hadn't completely allayed his curiosity. 'I'll be in first thing in the morning, though.'

'Chris must be very relieved. It's been hectic here these past few days. Mind you, it's always busy,' she replied, keeping the conversation flowing in the hope that it would distract him.

'So Chris was saying. From what I could gather, they were having problems keeping up even before Jonathan was taken ill,' he said levelly.

'Dr Wright told me that the lists have doubled since that new housing estate was built on the outskirts of town,' Beth explained, feeling easier now that the conversation was firmly centred on the practice.

'And that's probably been a contributing factor to why he's in hospital,' Adam said darkly. 'It appears that Jonathan has been having chest pains for some time, only he was too busy to go for a check-up. He self-diagnosed angina and has been treating himself for it.'

'I had no idea,' she exclaimed.

'Nobody had. Jonathan didn't want anyone to know because he was afraid that he might be forced to cut down the amount of work that he does. Aunt Mary only found out because he confessed to the specialist.'

He gave a deep laugh. 'I wouldn't like to be in his shoes when he gets out of hospital. Aunt Mary might be a gentle soul but I'm sure she'll make him pay for his deviousness!'

'I expect she'll forgive him in the end. She must be so relieved that he's going to be all right,' Beth said firmly.

Adam shrugged. 'I'm sure you're right. They have a great marriage. If anyone needs any tips on how to make a relationship work, they only need to look at that pair.'

'A good role model for you?' she suggested, suddenly curious about the state of Adam's own love life. He hadn't mentioned that he was married but suddenly the thought that he might have a wife and family was strangely unpalatable, and not just because it could have repercussions on what she wanted to ask him.

'Oh, I decided a long time ago that marriage wasn't for me. Once bitten, twice shy, as the saying goes.'

Beth frowned. That seemed to imply that he'd been let down at some point, and she couldn't help wondering if it had anything to do with her sister. Claire had always claimed that her relationship with Adam Knight had been strictly fun, but had he felt the same about it?

The idea troubled her. However, before she could try to find out more he suddenly sighed. 'Anyway, enough of all that. You must be itching to put your feet up for half an hour before evening surgery and here I am, rabbiting on. You're too good a listener, Beth. You remind me of Claire in that respect as well.'

She summoned a smile, although she couldn't deny that the comparison was disquieting. She had loved Claire and should have been pleased to be compared favourably to her, but the thought that Adam was measuring her against her sister troubled her.

'I shall take that as a compliment,' she said, refusing to dwell on the idea. There were far more pressing matters to focus on, but was this the right moment to tell him? He was obviously tired from all the travelling so maybe it would be better to leave it until tomorrow when he would be better able to cope with the news.

It was a relief to be able to put off the moment a while longer and she smiled at him. 'Right, I'm away upstairs for a cup of tea.'

'You're living in the flat over the surgery?' Adam asked in surprise.

'Yes. It was a real bonus because I couldn't have afforded

anywhere as big otherwise. A bedsit certainly wouldn't have
been suitable when—' She just managed to stop in time.
Adam looked at her curiously, his brows drawing together
into a slight frown.

'Why wouldn't a bedsit have been suitable?' he asked
flatly before an odd expression crossed his face. 'Sorry, I
didn't mean to pry. It's none of my business if you're living
with someone.'

'I'm not,' she admitted huskily because it still hurt to
recall what had happened. 'I was in a relationship for quite
some time but we split up a few months ago. That's why I
needed a place to live when I took the job in Winton. I
moved out of the house we'd been sharing after I broke off
our engagement.'

'Tough. It must have been a difficult time for you.'

Adam reached over and squeezed her hand in a genuine
show of sympathy, and for some reason she felt some of the
hurt dissolve. It was all very strange so that it was an effort
to reply calmly when he bade her goodbye.

Beth went up to the flat and made herself a cup of tea
then opened the back door. There was a flight of steps leading from the flat to the car park, with a small balcony at the
top. She'd filled some plastic tubs with colourful plants and
had bought a small bench seat from the local garden centre
and had arranged them out there.

It was her own little oasis of calm, the place she went to
when she wanted to think, and there was a lot to think about
at the moment, most of it centred on one person, funnily
enough—Adam Knight. The man she had searched for for
so long.

He wasn't anything like she had imagined he would be.

Evening surgery was packed. Even Eileen looked frazzled
by the end of the night. Chris Andrews looked positively
grey with fatigue when Beth bumped into him on her way
to the office.

'What a night!' he declared. 'Don't folk know that it's summer and that coughs, colds and other such nasties should have been left well behind by now?'

Beth smiled sympathetically. 'It's hard to believe that we could have an outbreak of flu at this time of the year. It's the start of the hay fever season soon.'

'Which means more running eyes and stuffy noses.' Chris sounded really downhearted. 'Sometimes I feel like packing in this job and going off beachcombing. There has to be more to life than this!'

'It should get better now that Adam is here,' she said, trying to sound encouraging because she could tell that Chris was down in the dumps.

'It should. I only wish he was staying here on a permanent basis, but this isn't his scene at all.' Chris shrugged when she looked at him. 'Adam has itchy feet and I can't see him ever settling down in any one place. He prefers the nomadic life—no ties, no commitments other than to his work. Mind you, I'm starting to think he has the right idea. I must have been mad to opt for the life of a GP!'

Chris didn't appear to expect her to say anything, thankfully enough. Beth went into the office and checked her list for the following morning, but she couldn't help thinking about what she had just heard. Not that it had come as a surprise. She had guessed a long time ago that Adam Knight was the type of man who avoided any kind of commitment. It made it that more difficult to assess how he would react to what she had to tell him.

It was a worrying thought but she tried to put it out of her head as she went up to the flat and changed out of her uniform. She was a little later than usual so she didn't waste time as she slipped on a pair of jeans and a sweatshirt, then pulled the pins out of her hair and quickly ran her fingers through it.

The gleaming red-gold strands swirled around her shoulders as she opened the back door, catching the last rays of evening sunlight. The light was so bright that her eyes were momentarily dazzled when she stepped onto the balcony and she didn't see the man who was sitting on the bench. It was only when he spoke that she realised he was there.

'Hello, Beth. I wonder if you could spare me a minute.'

She gasped and pressed a hand to her racing heart. 'You scared the wits out of me, Adam!'

'Sorry.' He stood up and looked pointedly at the door. 'Perhaps we could go back inside?'

Beth swallowed hard, wondering what it was about the way he was looking at her that made her feel so nervous. 'I was just on my way out. Can't it wait till tomorrow?'

'I'm afraid not. We've wasted most of a day as it is.' He sat back down on the bench although his eyes never left her face. 'It was you who phoned me this morning, wasn't it? I wish I had recognised your voice sooner but I was still rather hungover from the flight.'

He treated her to a cool smile when she didn't reply. 'If you're wondering how I discovered it had been you calling then you have the wonders of modern technology to thank. I'd forgotten to set the answering machine before I left this morning, you see. A stupid mistake, bearing in mind I was hoping that the airline would phone about my missing baggage.

'Anyway, I checked to see if there had been any calls by dialling one-four-seven-one, and there'd been just the one, first thing this morning. Aunt Mary keeps a list of numbers by the phone and, lo and behold, there it was—the number for the surgery flat. The bit of the puzzle I can't solve is why you were phoning me. Correct me if I'm wrong, but you did say that we hadn't met before today?'

'No we hadn't, but I…I've been trying to get in touch with you for a while,' she admitted shakily.

'I see. And are you going to tell me why? Or are we going to skirt around it for another day?' He laughed hollowly. 'I told you earlier that I had a feeling there was something I was missing. You denied it then but I do hope that you aren't going to try and deny it now?'

Her face stung at the mockery she heard in his voice. Maybe he didn't realise how difficult this was for her but she resented the fact that he saw fit to ridicule her. 'I apologise for lying to you. My only excuse is that it was a shock to have you turning up like that.'

She stared defiantly at him. 'As I told you before, I had no idea that you had any connections with the surgery. Claire never told me that.'

'Ah, yes, Claire. Funny how it all seems to come back to her. This is all to do with your sister, isn't it?'

He leant forward and Beth could see the tension that had grooved deep lines on either side of his mouth. 'I guessed that as soon as I worked out that it had been you phoning me this morning. It's the only link you and I have. I knew your sister very well at one time, Beth, as you know. However, I haven't seen her in years. So what possible reason could you have for seeking me out after all this time?'

Beth could feel her heart racing. The drumming beat was making her feel sick. So much hinged on how Adam took what she had to tell him that she was scared to death in case she made a mess of it.

She stared into his deep blue eyes, realising how familiar they were. Such a wonderful shade of blue, the thick black lashes that framed them simply highlighting the intensity of their colour...

She swung round and hurried back inside the flat then went straight to her bedroom. Adam was still sitting exactly where she had left him when she went outside again. The sun was lower in the sky now and his face was partly in shadow. It made it difficult to gauge his expression but she drove all thought of how he might react from her mind. She had to tell him the truth, no matter what happened afterwards!

'I want you to take a look at this,' she said huskily, her

voice quavering because the tension was almost palpable at that moment. She handed him the photograph then turned away, not wanting to see his reaction.

The sky was red and purple now, streaked with gold along the horizon as the sun slid from the sky. Maybe Claire was looking down on them from that sea of glorious colour, and if she was then Beth prayed that her sister would understand why she had no choice but to break her word.

'Who is she?'

She heard the tremor in his voice and her heart ached because she knew instinctively that he was going to find her answer painful. Maybe he *had* suspected why Claire had asked to see him all those years ago, but it was one thing to dismiss a suspicion and another to ignore a fact. There was a gentleness in her voice when she replied that she hadn't expected to hear there because suddenly she cared how he took this news, cared not just because of Hannah but because of Adam himself.

'Her name is Hannah and she's six years old. She's Claire's daughter.'

She heard his swift intake of breath but she couldn't stop, couldn't let herself think of anything else at that moment except what had to be done. 'She's your daughter, too, Adam.'

Afterwards, she was never sure if the silence had lasted only in her imagination. It seemed to run on and on yet even though she was physically aching to say something, she couldn't break it. She needed Adam to speak first so that she could decide how to handle the situation from that point on.

'I didn't know. I had no idea...'

Beth heard him take a deep breath but his voice was raw with pain and a host of things that made her eyes prickle with tears. 'Claire never told me. She never, ever told me!'

'I know she didn't.' She swung round, surprised by the need she felt to reassure him. His face was completely in shadow now but she saw the glitter of moisture on his cheeks and her heart quailed because of what else she had to tell him soon.

'Claire decided not to tell you in that letter she sent you but…'

'What letter?' he demanded immediately. 'I never received any letter.'

'Claire wrote to you when she found out that she was pregnant,' she said slowly. 'She didn't want to, but I persuaded her that she should.'

'I never received a letter from her,' he said, and his tone was so harsh and flat that Beth knew at once that he was telling her the truth. She shrugged, not sure what to say because this new development had shaken her. For all these years she had blamed him for not replying, suspected him of deliberately avoiding his responsibilities, yet suddenly she realised that she had been doing him an injustice. The crazy thing was how relieved she felt.

'I don't know what happened to it, then. All I know is that Claire wrote and asked if she could see you. She was going to tell you about the baby if she thought it was the best thing to do…'

'What do you mean *if* it was the best thing to do? It was my child, damn it! I had the right to know!'

Beth heard the anger in his voice and knew that she had to find a way to explain her sister's actions. 'She wanted to do what was right for everyone concerned…you, the baby and herself.'

'Really? How very good of her.' His anger rose on a sudden wave and seemed to envelop them both. 'What it boils down to is that she was going to sit in judgement on me, decide whether or not I was fit to be told that I had a child! How could that be right? You tell me that!'

'Don't! There's no point getting angry with Claire. She didn't do it to hurt you.'

It took just a couple of steps to reach the bench but Beth's heart was aching when she saw how tightly his fingers were clutching the photograph. Adam was angry but more importantly he was upset and she wanted to help him understand because it might help.

'You and Claire hadn't planned on having a child and she didn't want your whole life to be disrupted as a result of it. So she made the decision to try and find out how you would feel about the idea before she told you.'

'And decided when I didn't answer her letter that that was the end of it. It let her off the hook, didn't it? Gave her an excuse not to contact me again. I hadn't bothered replying so obviously I wasn't interested. Was that what you both thought?'

She sighed, wishing that she could deny it. 'She wasn't to know that you hadn't received the letter.'

'Maybe not. But surely the possibility should have occurred to her. Claire knew that I was planning on going overseas. It wouldn't take a genius to work out that the letter might not have reached me. She knew very well that she could have got in touch with me through my uncle, but she didn't make any attempt to do so, did she? She conveniently wrote me out of my child's life!'

Beth touched his hand and it felt icy despite the warmth of the evening air. 'All I can do is repeat what I've just told you, that Claire did what she thought was best. You must try to believe that.'

'It isn't easy. All these years and I never knew that I had a daughter.' He stared at the picture then ran his hand over his eyes. 'I can't seem to take it in. If you hadn't told me, I would never have known about her...'

He stopped and she felt his hand clench on the photograph. His voice seemed to grate when he continued, vibrating along her nerves, filling her with apprehension. 'Why did you tell me? You said that you'd spent a long time tracking me down but why now? You could have told me when your sister died, or at any point during these past seven years, but you didn't. So why did you suddenly decide that it was time I knew about Hannah?'

Beth removed her hand abruptly. This was the really difficult part and she wasn't sure that she could deal with it.

Only she had no choice.

'Because Hannah desperately needs your help,' she explained huskily, struggling to keep control of her emotions. 'Six months ago she started being ill, you see. She was tired and listless all the time. At first I wondered if it was a reaction to Claire's death even though she seemed to have accepted it.'

She knew that she was laying the ground, trying to lessen the shock so she continued when he didn't say anything. 'I was so worried about her that I took her to the doctor and he ordered some tests to be done. When the results came back they showed that Hannah had acute lymphoblastic leukaemia.'

'God!' He stood up and paced to the top of the steps then swung round. 'How has she responded to treatment? I take it that she's in hospital?'

'Very well and, yes, she is in hospital. She's been in St Jude's for several months now,' she explained quietly.

'And what's the prognosis? Has the consultant said what her chances are?' he rapped out.

Beth sensed that he needed to hear all the facts to help him deal with the shock he'd had. 'Mr Guest—that's Hannah's consultant—is very pleased with her. He's confident that she'll be in remission soon.'

'Thank heaven for that!' He took a deep breath and she saw a shudder run through him. 'So what happens next?'

'Once remission is achieved then, hopefully, Hannah will have a bone-marrow transplant. Apparently, they do that straight away nowadays once a child is in remission.'

She paused, choosing her words with care because this part was so important. 'The problem is that the hospital hasn't found a suitable donor for her. They've gone through all the usual channels and I've been tested, but they've drawn a blank. I was hoping that if I did manage to find you, you might be willing to be tested. I know it's a lot to ask…'

She stopped when he swore under his breath. He turned back to her and the expression on his face made her tremble because it was so ferocious. Her heart turned over because she couldn't bear it if he refused.

'It's her only chance, Adam! If Hannah doesn't get this bone-marrow transplant then her chances of survival are virtually nil. Please, say that you'll think about it.'

'I don't need to think about it! What kind of a man do you think I am?' His blue eyes seemed to burn with an inner fire as he glared at her. 'This is my child we're talking about—my daughter. I'd give up my life if it would help her!'

'You mean that you'll do it? You'll be tested?' It was almost too much to take in. She stared at him and saw an expression of intense pain cross his face.

'Yes. And now I want to see her. I take it that you were going to the hospital to visit Hannah, so I'll go with you. I've got Uncle Jonathan's car so I'll drive.'

'Oh, but…' she began, not sure that it would be wise to rush into a meeting between the pair that night. Adam needed time to come to terms with what she had told him and she needed to prepare Hannah.

He was halfway down the steps but he stopped. 'No buts, Beth. I want to see Hannah. I've missed the first six years of her life so I think I have the right to do that.'

She couldn't argue with that and didn't try because she knew it would be pointless. 'All right. But I want you to understand that Hannah doesn't know anything about you. Claire…well, Claire decided that it was better not to tell her in the circumstances.'

'And you agreed to keep the secret, didn't you?' He smiled thinly. 'You and Claire erased me from Hannah's life

but the situation is going to change from here on, believe
me.'

'What do you mean?'

'That I intend to make up for all those lost years. Hannah
needs a father. She needs me in more ways than you ever
realised!'

He turned and ran down the steps and a few seconds later
she heard a car starting up. She quickly locked the door and
followed him, deeply troubled by what he had said.

He had a right to be angry, a right even to blame her for
keeping her promise to Claire, but did he have the right to
disrupt Hannah's life? How would the child feel if she grew
fond of him then he upped and left again? Chris had told
her that Adam had an aversion to commitment, yet the one
thing a child needed was stability. Claire must have known
how Adam had felt all those years ago, which was why she
had been so loath to tell him about Hannah. Could she really
trust him not to break her precious niece's heart?

She slid into the passenger seat and glanced at Adam as
he put the car into gear, felt a little bubble of panic rise to
the surface of her mind. Could she trust him not to break
her own heart as well?

Now, where had *that* thought sprung from?

CHAPTER THREE

THERE WERE still a lot of parents around when they arrived at the hospital. St Jude's had an open door policy in its children's wards and there were few restrictions on visiting times.

Beth called in at least twice a day to see Hannah and would have gone more often if she'd had the time because she loved being with her niece. However, her footsteps slowed as they approached the doors to the ward. Adam hadn't said a word to her on the drive to the hospital and she needed to know what he intended to do before she introduced him to Hannah.

'Look, Adam, I know this has been a shock for you but I want you to promise me that you won't do anything…well, hasty.'

He paused to look at her and she shivered when she caught the full force of his icy stare. 'What you really mean is that you don't want me to tell Hannah who I am. Isn't that right, Beth?'

'Yes.' She forced herself to meet his eyes, refusing to dwell on why she felt so guilty. She had made a promise to Claire so she shouldn't feel bad about not having told him about Hannah sooner. 'Hannah doesn't know anything about you. If you go in there and blurt out who you are, you'll simply confuse her. She's only six, Adam, and she's been through a lot in this past year.'

'And you really think that I don't understand that?' He smiled grimly when she shrugged. 'Obviously not. After all, you know very little about me, do you, Beth? I don't suppose you cared enough to find out. However, you can stop worrying. I think I have a bit more sensitivity than to an-

35

nounce to a sick child that I'm the father she never knew she had.'

She winced when she heard the anger in his voice. 'I know this isn't easy for you, Adam,' she began but he curtly interrupted her.

'Spare me the sympathy. Now, are you coming or shall I go and find Hannah by myself?'

He didn't wait for her to reply as he pushed open the door. Beth led the way, feeling sick with nerves because she still wasn't sure how he was going to handle this meeting. Hannah had always been shy with strangers and she'd grown even more introverted since her mother had died. Although she seemed to have accepted the nurses and doctors with whom she came into daily contact, Beth knew how quickly the little girl could clam up with someone new. Would Adam understand that and make allowances?

Beth's nerves felt as taut as violin strings as she led the way to Hannah's bed. The staff had tried to make the ward as child-friendly as possible by covering the walls with posters and using colourful linen on the beds rather than the regulation hospital white. However, there was no escaping from the fact that the children in there were very sick.

Out of the corner of her eye she saw Adam's head turn as they passed one child after another. Most were hooked up to drips that were pumping potent cocktails of chemicals into their small bodies. All the children in the ward had cancer in one form or another and they were treated with a vast array of drugs.

Some were designed to destroy the cancerous cells, others to protect against infection, always a major concern. Then there were the transfusions of blood and platelets they all needed at regular intervals. It could be a little overwhelming to someone visiting the ward for the first time.

'All these kids…' Adam took a deep breath but she could see the pain in his eyes when he looked at her. 'I never realised that there were so many children suffering like this.'

'It does come as a shock, even when you work in medicine,' she agreed softly. She caught sight of Hannah and waved, feeling her nerves tighten that little bit more when she felt Adam stiffen. Without stopping to think, she caught hold of his hand and squeezed it.

'It will be fine, you'll see. Just don't worry if Hannah doesn't say much to you. She's very shy at first with strangers.'

He winced at that and Beth could have bitten her tongue for her lack of tact. Letting go of his hand, she quickly went to the child's bed and bent down to kiss her.

'Hello, darling. I'm sorry I'm late. It was really busy tonight at the surgery and I got held up.'

She ran her hand lightly over the child's head, feeling the prickle of stubble under her fingers. Hannah's hair had fallen out because of the drugs she had been receiving. It would grow again once she had completed her treatment, but Beth still grieved for the loss of the beautiful black curls because they had been a symbol of the fit and healthy child that her niece had been once upon a time.

Now as she turned to Adam and caught the fleeting expression of anguish on his face she knew that he was remembering the photograph she had shown him earlier. What a shock it must be for him to compare that child with the one in the bed. Unconsciously, her tone softened.

'Adam, I'd like you to meet Hannah. Come and say hello to her.'

She stepped aside so that he could approach the bed. He moved slowly, smiling at the child as he bent down and took her thin little hand in his large one and gravely shook it.

'Hello, Hannah. I hope you don't mind me coming to see you. Aunty Beth told me all about you, you see, and I asked her if I could visit you.'

Beth felt a lump come to her throat when she heard the tenderness in his voice. She realised that she was holding her breath as she waited to see how Hannah would respond.

'Are you and Aunty Beth friends?' Hannah asked, staring up at him with huge, curious blue eyes, eyes that were exactly the same colour as Adam's were.

'That's right, sweetheart.' He gave the child another warm smile and, surprisingly, she smiled back.

'That's OK, then,' she said with a worldly wisdom that made them both laugh.

Adam glanced at Beth and she saw the relief in his eyes and knew that he had been as worried as she had been about this first meeting. Realising it, it helped to allay her fears so that she found herself able to relax. Adam wouldn't deliberately do anything that might harm her precious niece.

'So, what did you do this afternoon, poppet?' she asked, moving a chair closer to the bed so that she could sit down. She was very conscious of Adam standing behind her, his arms folded across his broad chest as he listened while the little girl related everything she had done since Beth had seen her at lunchtime. When he shifted slightly, she found herself jumping nervously and had to force herself to concentrate on what Hannah was saying.

'What sort of a picture did you draw, Hannah?' Adam asked after Hannah had finished telling them about the lessons she had done that afternoon. The children were in hospital for such a long time that they had a teacher who came each day to keep them up to date with their school work. Hannah had drawn a picture that day as part of her work.

'I'll show you if you like,' the little girl offered shyly. 'See.'

She picked up a piece of paper from her bedside locker and gave it to him to look at. Beth felt her pulse leap when he leant forward to take it from the child and his arm brushed hers. She had been so keyed up before that she hadn't noticed that he'd changed out of the clothes he'd been wearing earlier. Now she found herself drinking in the sight of his lean muscular body clad in well-washed denim jeans and a faded black T-shirt. She couldn't help thinking how good he looked in the casual outfit, so much better than Ian had ever looked in his expensive suits.

The thought surprised her but she quickly dismissed it. She glanced at the picture that Adam was holding and laughed when she saw what her niece had drawn.

'Is that what I think it is, young lady?' she teased, pointing to a spot in the bottom right-hand corner of the drawing.

Adam raised his brows when Hannah giggled. 'What's the joke? Come on, don't be meanies—tell me what's so funny.'

Beth smiled as she looked at her niece. 'This little madam keeps hinting that she wants a dog for her birthday and she doesn't miss any opportunity to remind me about it. Every time she draws a picture she manages to *sneak* a dog into it somewhere!'

Adam chuckled when she pointed to a strange-looking creature in the corner of the picture. It was obvious that he hadn't realised what it was meant to be but he tactfully didn't say so. 'Ah, I see. It looks like it could be a Labrador to me. When is your birthday, Hannah?'

'Next month. I'll be seven,' Hannah informed him importantly.

Beth saw his face cloud over and hurriedly cut in. She knew that he must be thinking about all the years that he'd missed. 'If anyone in the ward has a birthday the nurses give them a party. I expect they'll give you one, too, poppet. Won't that be fun?'

'S'pose so,' the child agreed wistfully. 'But it won't be as much fun as last year when Mummy gave me a party and all my friends from school came.'

Beth bit back a sigh because there was little she could say to contradict that. Fortunately, Rose Johnson, one of the staff nurses on the ward, came to check Hannah's drip just then so the child was distracted.

'That's fine,' Rose said when she had finished. Beth had met Rose when they'd done their training together and they had been firm friends ever since. She suspected that there had been an ulterior motive as to why Rose had chosen to check the drip at that precise moment, and she was proved right when her friend looked pointedly at Adam.

'I see that you've got another visitor tonight, Hannah. Aren't you going to introduce me?'

'This is Adam and he's a friend of Aunty Beth's,' the child explained, and for some reason Beth found herself blushing.

'Is he indeed?' Rose treated Beth to an old-fashioned look before she turned to smile at Adam. 'Nice to meet you, Adam. Will we be seeing more of you around here in the future?'

Beth glared at her friend but Rose pretended not to notice. Fortunately, Adam seemed unaware of any undercurrents. 'You can be sure of it,' he replied evenly. 'I shall be a regular visitor from now on.'

Rose's brows rose. 'Really? Well, I'll look forward to seeing you again, then.'

Beth glared at her friend as Rose turned to leave but all she got in return was a smug smile. She sighed as she watched Rose making her way down the ward. She'd bet a pound to a penny that she knew what her friend was thinking, but Rose was wrong! Adam might have gone along with Hannah's innocent introduction but did he really see himself as her friend? Could he ever be that when he blamed her as much as he blamed Claire for keeping the child's existence a secret?

It was an oddly painful thought and Beth found it difficult to put it out of her mind while she chatted to Hannah. When she noticed that the child was beginning to tire, she stood up, glad to be able to bring the visit to an end. Introducing Adam to Hannah was bound to have been difficult for all of them but things should get easier from now on, she assured herself.

'It's time you were asleep, sweetheart. I'll see you tomorrow.' She bent and kissed the little girl. 'Night-night, sleep tight. Mind the bed bugs—'

'Don't bite,' Hannah finished for her, yawning widely. Her lids were already starting to droop as Beth moved away from the bed but they suddenly shot up as she looked at Adam. 'Will you come to see me tomorrow as well, Adam?'

'Of course I will.' He stepped forward and after the tiniest hesitation brushed the child's pale cheek with his lips. 'Goodnight, Hannah. Sweet dreams.'

'Night-night, Adam.'

Hannah's eyes had closed before they were halfway down the ward. Adam paused by the door to look back and Beth could tell what an effort it cost him to contain his feelings.

'She's so tiny and frail, isn't she? She looks as though a puff of wind would blow her away,' he said thickly.

'She's stronger than you think, a real little fighter. The fact that she's got this far is a measure of her spirit,' she told him softly, knowing what he must be going through.

'She still has a long way to go, though. Even if she has this bone-marrow transplant there are no guarantees that she will pull through.'

Beth heard the pain in his voice and wanted with all her heart to reassure him, but it would have been wrong to lie.

'No, there are no guarantees but we can't afford to think like that, Adam. We have to be positive and convince ourselves that the transplant will work.' She shrugged when he looked at her. 'When hope is all you have then it becomes doubly important that you never lose sight of it.'

'It can't have been easy for you these past months, Beth.' He opened the door for her, stopping once again when they were out in the corridor. His blue eyes were intent as he searched her face. Beth had the funniest feeling that he was trying to look deep inside her mind and looked away, unsure why the idea disturbed her so much.

'It hasn't been. But it's been much worse for Hannah. She's the one who has lost her mother and is now fighting for her life,' she replied huskily. She had only met Adam a few short hours ago so why should she imagine that he could read her mind?

'But you're the one who has had to be strong. The one who has had to live with this nightmare day after day.' He took hold of her hands and gripped them hard. 'Thank you, Beth. Thank you for everything that you've done for Hannah.'

Beth felt herself choke up and quickly withdrew her hands. 'You'll have me crying all over you if you keep on like that,' she admonished with a shaky laugh. 'And I'm quite sure *that's* something you want to avoid!'

'Heavens, yes!' He feigned horror as he glanced down. 'You might start crying all over this T-shirt and that would never do. The thought of the damage all those salty tears could cause sends shudders down my spine!'

Beth chuckled, grateful for his attempts to lighten the mood. 'I can imagine. You need to be very careful with *antique* fabric like that.'

'I hope that wasn't meant as a criticism. I'll have you know that this T-shirt is priceless. I defy you to find another one like it!'

His smile was unashamedly teasing as he started walking along the corridor. Beth felt her spirits lift when she looked at his laughing face. Maybe it was crazy, but just knowing that Adam was going to be around seemed to have taken some of the burden off her shoulders.

'Priceless? Well, I certainly wouldn't want to guess how much it's worth,' she retorted. She was still smiling as they rounded a corner on their way to the lifts and almost collided with the man who was coming in the opposite direction.

'Oops, sorry...!' she began then found her voice drying up when she realised that it was her ex-fiancé, Ian Patterson.

'Hello, Beth. Fancy running into you like this,' he said with a distinctly unpleasant smile. 'How's the new job going? You're not sorry yet that you decided to leave the bright city lights behind?'

'Not at all. I'm really enjoying working at the surgery,' she replied stiffly. She hadn't seen Ian for some time but the memory of what had happened between them still rankled. After Claire had died, she had taken Hannah to live with her and Ian, confident that he'd shared her desire to give the child a secure and loving home. However, it hadn't taken her long to realise that she'd made a huge mistake.

Now she tilted her chin and stared defiantly at him. 'Hannah is fine, by the way. I'm sure you were going to ask about her so I'll save you the trouble.'

'You already know my views on that subject,' he replied bluntly. 'If you choose to waste your life by looking after someone else's kid then that's your business.'

He glanced at Adam and she saw an expression of disdain cross his face as he took stock of the other man's appearance. It was obvious when Ian turned away without uttering a word that he intended to ignore him. However, it appeared that wasn't what Adam wanted.

'Aren't you going to introduce us, Beth? Never mind, I'll do it for you. I'm Adam Knight.' Adam held out his hand. Beth saw Ian hesitate before he reluctantly shook it.

It struck her then that she had never realised just what a snob Ian was. She had always known that he was ambitious and that his aim was to mix with the very top levels of society. She had found it rather endearing, in fact, a tiny flaw in his otherwise perfect character. However, now she could see that there was nothing endearing about the way Ian looked down on people whom he considered inferior.

'Sorry, I didn't catch your name?' Adam's tone was so courteous that she couldn't explain the shiver that crept down her spine. She shot him a wary glance but there was nothing about the polite smile he gave Ian to confirm her suspicions that he was up to something.

'Ian Patterson, senior registrar on the coronary care unit.

Basically, it means that I'm in charge of the unit for most of the time,' Ian stated pompously.

'Really?' Adam looked impressed. Beth saw Ian start to relax, confident that he was on safe ground. However, she had a horrible feeling that he was going to regret that rather large distortion of the truth. Although Ian's position was a senior one, he was one of three registrars on the coronary care unit, and by no means the head of the team.

'You must have to shoulder an awful lot of responsibility in a job like that,' Adam continued in a tone that simply invited confidences. 'It must be terribly stressful at times.'

'I suppose it can be if you're that type of person,' Ian replied, positively preening under all the interest. 'However, making life and death decisions comes easier to some than it does to others.'

'I see. Obviously you find it easy—to make life-and-death decisions, I mean,' Adam said mildly.

Beth bit her lip because she didn't know whether to laugh or admonish him for the way he was leading Ian on. Couldn't Ian see that he was being led like a lamb to the slaughter? Apparently not!

'Oh, yes. I have no difficulty at all with that. The trick is to take a dispassionate view. Unfortunately, far too many doctors get emotionally involved with the people they treat.' Ian was getting into his stride now as he expounded his views. 'That's a big mistake. One needs to think of them merely as cases. That way you can do your job far more efficiently.'

'And James feels the same as you do?' Adam inserted smoothly.

'James?' Ian repeated, before he suddenly paled. 'You know James Dickinson, the consultant on Coronary Care?'

'Yes. Sorry, didn't I mention it before?' Adam laughed deeply. 'James and I go way back. We were at Guys together as housemen. We still keep in touch. In fact, I'm hoping to get together with him in the next couple of weeks. I must remember to mention that I met you. Patterson, wasn't it? Senior registrar?'

'I…um. Yes. Fine. Well, if you'll excuse me.' Ian hurried away, still muttering.

Beth took a deep breath and somehow managed to contain her mirth until they were safely inside the lift. 'Oh, that was wonderful! I can't believe that you did that, Adam. I can't believe that Ian fell for it either!'

Adam smiled as the lift whizzed them down to the ground floor. 'Everyone needs taking down a peg or two occasionally. Some deserve it more than others.'

'Ian definitely deserved it! I can't understand why I never realised how pompous and self-opinionated he is,' she admitted ruefully. The lift reached the ground floor just then so they got out and walked towards the exit.

'People always say that love is blind. I think that can apply to character as well as appearance,' Adam observed as they left the building and walked back to the car.

Night had drawn in now and the light had dimmed to a blue-grey opalescence. There were few people about at that hour and those they passed seemed more concerned with their own affairs. It was a moment that simply invited confidences and Beth found herself suddenly eager to pour out the whole miserable story.

'I must have been blind to imagine that Ian was the man I wanted to spend my life with.'

'So Patterson was the guy you split up from recently?' Adam asked quietly. They had reached the end of the path and a little way to their right there was a small garden area with an arbour containing a wooden bench. When he led her towards it, she didn't object.

'Yes. I went out with Ian for almost two years. We got engaged about this time last year, in fact, just a month before Claire was killed.' She sighed as she sat down and stared at the velvety black sky. 'I thought I was the luckiest woman alive when Ian asked me to marry him.'

'What went wrong?' Adam asked. He crossed his legs and leant back against the hard wooden slats, obviously wanting to hear the whole story. Beth found herself wondering fleetingly why he was interested but the urge to get it all off her chest was too strong to resist.

'After Claire died I brought Hannah home to live with us. Ian and I had bought a house a few months earlier so we had plenty of room.' She shrugged. 'It never entered my head that Ian wouldn't like the idea of her living with us.'

'Where did he think she would live?' he interjected.

'I've no idea. He knew that I was the only family Claire had. I don't think that he cared so long as he didn't have to be responsible for her.'

'It can't have been easy for Claire, bringing up Hannah on her own.'

'I don't suppose it was,' Beth replied gently because she'd heard the remorse in his voice. Adam had known nothing about Hannah at that time so he shouldn't blame himself for not having been there to help. However, she knew that it was going to take him time to come to terms with what had happened, then wondered why that thought caused her such pain.

'Anyway, Hannah seemed to settle down with us reasonably well,' she continued, not giving herself time to dwell on it. 'She was a bit clingy at first but that was to be expected. I suggested that I should reduce the number of hours I worked, but Ian was totally against it.'

Her mouth compressed as she thought about the arguments they'd had. 'It would have meant me taking a cut in salary and he didn't see why we should alter our lifestyle to fit in with a child. That's when I realised that we had major problems.'

'I see. So what brought things to a head?' Adam asked, his voice rumbling through the darkness. Beth glanced at him again but his face was just a blur now that the last of the light had faded. She had no idea what he was thinking at that moment.

'Ian wanted us to go away for Christmas with some of his friends. Hannah wasn't well by that point and he knew that I was worried about her, but he just dismissed my concerns as fussing.' Her voice hardened. 'When I found out that she had leukaemia and needed urgent treatment, he was more concerned about losing the deposit on the holiday than the fact that she was seriously ill. Incredible, isn't it?'

'Incredible isn't the word I'd use,' Adam said harshly. She heard him take a deep breath as though he was struggling to keep control, not that she blamed him for being angry. She still felt angry herself whenever she thought about how Ian had behaved.

'What happened after that?' he asked after a couple of seconds had elapsed.

'Ian told me that he wasn't prepared to put his life on hold for the sake of a child who wasn't his. He gave me an ultimatum—either I put Hannah into care or we went our separate ways.' She gave a disgusted laugh. 'He honestly thought that I'd choose him over Hannah!'

'A lot of women would have done, Beth. Not everyone would want to take on the responsibility of a sick child.'

She was shaking her head before he had finished speaking. 'There was never any question about what I wanted to do. I love Hannah and I intend to be there for her for as long as she needs me.'

'It's easy to say that now, but how about in the future? What happens if you meet someone else who feels the same as Ian did?'

He turned to face her and even through the darkness she could see the determination that lit his eyes. 'It all boils down to one simple fact, Beth—Hannah isn't your child. She's mine.'

CHAPTER FOUR

'WHAT do you mean?' Beth whispered hoarsely. She felt her heart leap when Adam stood up and strode to the edge of the path. She found herself gripping the arm of the bench so hard that her fingers ached as she waited for him to answer.

'That I appreciate everything you've done for Hannah but she's no longer your responsibility. I'm her father, Beth, and it's about time that I took care of her.'

He swung round and she saw the determination on his face. 'Why should you have all the worry of looking after her from now on? Hannah is my daughter and I intend to make up for all the years that I've missed.'

Beth rose to her feet, aware that she was trembling. The last thing she wanted was for them to start arguing when they should be working together, but it seemed there was no way to avoid it. He couldn't honestly believe that it would be right to take Hannah away from her!

'I understand how you feel, Adam. Really I do,' she began, trying to remain calm.

'I doubt it. I don't think you have any idea how I feel,' he said harshly, so harshly that she flinched. 'I know you explained why your sister decided not to tell me immediately about Hannah, but there's no excuse for what she did. I had a *right* to know that I had a child, just as Hannah had the right to know that she had a father!'

Beth didn't know what to say. Adam was only stating what she had thought so many times in the past. Now she felt overwhelmed by guilt for the part she had played in keeping Hannah's existence a secret from him.

'Claire honestly and truly thought that she was doing the

right thing,' she explained numbly, feeling that she had to defend her sister and, indirectly, herself.

'Well, I'm afraid she got it wrong. And there's nothing you can say that will convince me otherwise.' His tone was unyielding. 'Now, I think it's time we went home. Frankly, I'm too tired to discuss this any more tonight.'

He turned and strode back up the path. Beth followed him, wishing that she could think of something to say to ease the situation. However, it was going to take more than a few soothing words to make him understand that Claire hadn't deliberately set out to hurt him.

She sighed as it struck her that she might have touched upon the real crux of the problem. Adam seemed very bitter about the fact that Claire hadn't tried harder to contact him and it just didn't gel with what her sister had always claimed about their affair not having been serious.

Could the real truth be that Adam had wanted the relationship to continue and it had been Claire who had broken it off? It would explain Claire's reluctance to contact him when she'd found out she was pregnant, and why she hadn't made any further effort to trace him when he hadn't replied to her letter. Maybe Claire had known all along that Adam was in love with her and had wanted to avoid hurting him any more than she already had.

It made sense even though Beth found herself strangely reluctant to accept the idea. She didn't like to think that Adam might still be in love with Claire, strangely enough.

'Right, Mr Hopkins, if you could step onto the scales then I can see how much weight you've lost since last week.'

It was only midway through morning surgery but Beth was already starting to flag. She had spent a restless night going over everything that had happened the day before and had fallen asleep just as dawn had been breaking. Consequently, she'd had to drag herself out of bed when her alarm had rung and had felt tired and sluggish all morning.

So far she'd managed to avoid Adam. She'd had patients booked in early that morning so she'd been busy when he'd arrived. However, she knew that at some point she would have to try to resolve the situation that had arisen the night before. The trouble was that she had no idea how she was going to convince him that he couldn't disrupt Hannah's life by claiming parental rights.

'If you wouldn't mind, Nurse. I do have other things to do today.'

She returned her mind to the job at hand and smiled placatingly at her patient. Roger Hopkins was a local businessman in his fifties. Eileen had told her that he owned The Willows, a hugely popular hotel and restaurant in the centre of the town.

He'd come to the surgery a few weeks earlier, complaining of shortness of breath. Dr Wright had given him a thorough examination but hadn't found anything seriously wrong. He had concluded that Roger Hopkins's problems stemmed from the fact that he was overweight and a heavy smoker. He'd put him on a diet and had advised him to stop smoking. Beth doubted whether the man had heeded at least part of the advice when she checked the reading on the scales.

'I'm afraid that you've gained two pounds since I last saw you, Mr Hopkins. Are you sure that you're sticking to the diet?'

'I don't have time for all that nonsense,' he blustered, puffing as he stepped off the scales and bent down to fasten his shoelaces. 'I have a business to run and it certainly wouldn't look good if I picked at my food when I'm entertaining clients.'

'But it's not doing your health any good to ignore Dr Wright's advice,' she countered gently. 'He recommended that you should try to lose at least a stone, and so far you've gained three pounds.'

'Your scales can't be right. I'm sure that I can't have

gained any weight,' he replied sharply, glaring at Beth as though it was her fault.

'I don't think so, Mr Hopkins. These scales are checked regularly for accuracy.' She smiled calmly at him, unruffled by his belligerent tone, and he had the grace to blush.

'Yes, well, I suppose I have been a little lax about it all. Since my wife died, I find that I'm spending more time than ever at work so I tend to eat in the restaurant there. It's better than going home to an empty house, you understand.'

'I do,' she agreed sympathetically. 'Do you have a family, Mr Hopkins?'

'A son, but I haven't seen him for a long time.' Roger Hopkins sighed. 'We had an argument a few years ago. We're too alike, you see. We both find it difficult to admit when we're wrong. Anyway, Martin walked out of the house, swearing that he wouldn't be coming back, and I've not heard a word from him since.'

'What a shame. Don't you have any idea where he's living? Maybe you could get in touch with him and see if you can clear up the misunderstanding,' Beth suggested.

'I've thought about it a lot, especially since Margaret died. The trouble is that I have no idea where to start,' the man explained sadly. 'The last I heard was that Martin was on his way to India. That's what we argued about, in fact. He wanted to take a year out after university to go travelling and I thought it was a waste of time. It isn't easy being a parent and sometimes you get it wrong. The problem is that you don't realise your mistakes until it's too late. Anyway, I'll try harder to stick to the diet, Nurse. All it takes is a bit more determination.'

'That's all,' Beth agreed. She sighed as he left, thinking how right he'd been about it being difficult to be a good parent. Claire had been a wonderful mother to Hannah but had she been right not to tell the child about her father?

It was impossible to answer that question so she tried not to dwell on it. She saw two more patients for routine blood-pressure checks then Eileen rang through to tell her that her next appointment had been cancelled. Beth was just thinking gratefully that she would be able to snatch a much-needed cup of coffee when Adam tapped on her door.

She felt her heart turn over as she wondered what he wanted. From the look of the shadows under his eyes she suspected that he hadn't slept any better than she had done. She wasn't sure if she was ready to face a continuation of the conversation they had begun the night before. However, it appeared that Adam's mind was focused strictly on work for the moment.

'I've got a patient with me, a Mrs Dwyer,' he told her as he came into the room and closed the door. 'Her daughter brought her in and I'm not at all happy with her. How fast can we get a blood test done?'

Beth frowned. 'We normally send bloods away to the lab and it's a couple of days before we get the results back. I suppose we could ask them to rush it through, but it would be this afternoon at the earliest before they got back to us.'

'That's too long. I'm working on a hunch here because I've not actually seen a case like this before. However, I'm pretty confident that Mrs Dwyer is suffering from Wernicke-Korsakoff syndrome.'

'Isn't that some sort of brain disorder?' Beth queried.

'That's right. It's caused by a deficiency of thiamine, which affects the brain and nervous system. It's the result of a poor diet combined with a defect in thiamine metabolism,' he explained. 'It's almost always linked to chronic alcohol dependence, which is what I suspect has caused this patient's problems.'

'What has the daughter told you?'

'Nothing. I've tried to tactfully broach the subject that her mother might have a drink problem, but the daughter won't discuss it.' He shook his head. 'People don't seem to realise that alcohol dependency is an illness and not something they should be too ashamed to talk about.'

'Difficult situation,' she sympathised. 'What are the mother's symptoms? I've heard about the disease but that's as far as it goes, I'm afraid.'

'Fortunately, it isn't all that common. However, it does make it harder to diagnose Wernicke's when you haven't seen many cases of it, and especially when you can't get a complete patient history,' he said worriedly. 'Mrs Dwyer is showing signs of nystagmus—those strange, jerky eye movements—plus she's obviously having trouble co-ordinating when she's walking. And she seems to have lost a lot of sensation in her hands and feet, and her reflexes are virtually nil.'

'And those are all symptoms of the disease, I imagine. So how can I help you?' Beth asked, understanding why he was so concerned.

'If you could have a word with the daughter and see if you can get anything out of her, it would be a real help.' He gave her a warm smile. 'She might respond better to you, Beth. You have that sort of effect on people, make them want to confide in you.'

'I was only thinking the same about you last night,' she said in surprise, then realised how revealing that had been and blushed.

'Thank you. It's good to hear that, especially after the way I behaved last night.' His tone was rueful. 'I think I came on a bit strong and I apologise for it.'

Did that mean he had changed his mind about wanting to take sole responsibility for Hannah? she wondered. However, before she could ask, he turned to leave.

'I'll send Hilary Dwyer in to see you. See what you can find out, will you? If it is Wernicke-Korsakoff syndrome then the mother is going to need immediate treatment. The next stage of the disease is severe memory loss, and it's irreversible if the patient doesn't receive prompt treatment.'

'How do you treat it?' she asked curiously.

'With high doses of intravenous thiamine. The symptoms

can be reversed in a couple of hours as long as it's caught in time. In fact, I'm going to ring for an ambulance and have her admitted to hospital rather than take any chances,' he announced, making up his mind. 'It would just be a help if I had some solid facts to back up my diagnosis.'

'Leave it with me,' she assured him. 'I'll do my best.'

'I know you will.' He gave her another of those wonderfully warm smiles before he left. Beth took a small breath, wondering how a smile could have such an effect on her. A few seconds of Adam Knight's magic and she could cope with anything!

Anything? that irritating voice whispered. Did that include all the problems she might have convincing him that Hannah's life shouldn't be disrupted?

She sighed as the feeling of warmth abruptly evaporated. It was going to take more than a smile to help her over that particular hurdle.

'I really don't know why I need to see you, Nurse. It isn't me who's ill, it's my mother!'

Beth smiled soothingly at the woman. Hilary Dwyer was a woman in her forties. Although she was neatly dressed, her clothes were extremely old-fashioned for a woman of her age. She had looked very agitated when Eileen had shown her in and had refused to sit down when Beth had offered her a seat.

'It's your mother we're concerned about.' Beth sat down, not wanting to appear to be crowding the woman by remaining standing by the door. 'Dr Knight wants to help her but he can't do that unless he finds out what has made her ill.'

'I've already told him everything I know! When I got home from the shops this morning, Mother wasn't well. I don't know what else I can tell him.' Hilary turned to the door. 'Now, if that's all…'

'Dr Knight thinks that your mother might have Wernicke-

Korsakoff syndrome. It's a very serious illness and if he's right she needs immediate treatment.'

Beth knew that she was taking a chance by being so blunt but she felt that she had no choice. 'It can be a side-effect of alcohol dependency, although that isn't the only cause. I understand how difficult it is to speak about something like that but it would help if we were in possession of all the facts. We need to know what we're dealing with.'

'Why that's ridiculous!' Hilary protested, but Beth saw the colour wash up her face and knew that Adam had been right in his suspicions.

'Alcoholism is an illness,' she explained gently. 'It isn't something to be ashamed of.'

Hilary blinked hard. 'I'm afraid that there aren't many people who would agree with you.'

'If you're worried about people finding out, please, understand that anything you tell me or Dr Knight is strictly confidential,' Beth said quickly. 'But if you want to do what's best for your mother then you must help us.'

Hilary Dwyer seemed to crumple all of a sudden. Beth got up and put an arm around the woman's shaking shoulders and helped her to a chair. 'It's been a nightmare,' Hilary admitted between sobs. 'I've tried so hard to take care of Mother but she's got worse. I don't know if I can cope much longer!'

The whole story poured out after that. Beth sighed as she listened to the poor woman's tale of the struggle she'd had to hide her mother's drinking problem from their friends and neighbours. If only Hilary had sought help instead of trying to cover up what had been going on, Beth thought. But maybe it was wrong to make a judgement like that. Most people did what they thought was best—as she and Claire had done.

She tried to put that last thought to the back of her mind as she went to have a word with Adam. He came to the door when she tapped on it and listened intently while she repeated what Hilary had told her.

'So I was right.' He sighed as he glanced back into the room. Mrs Dwyer was lying on the couch and didn't seem to be aware of what was going on around her. 'It's a shame the daughter didn't ask for help sooner. It can't have been easy for her if the situation has been going on for some time.'

'I'm sure it hasn't been. Is the ambulance on its way?' Beth asked flatly because she couldn't rid herself of the thought that she and Claire had made a mistake, even though she had gone along with her sister's wishes reluctantly.

'It should be here any minute.' He stopped her when she turned to leave. 'Are you all right, Beth?' He suddenly frowned. 'It's not Hannah, is it?'

'No, she's fine,' she said quickly, hearing the worry in his voice. 'I phoned the hospital this morning and she had a good night's sleep.'

'Thank heavens for that.' He sighed heavily. 'I can't believe that this time yesterday I didn't even know Hannah existed. Now I find that I can't get her out of my mind.'

He looked round when Eileen appeared to tell him that the ambulance had arrived. Beth quickly excused herself and went to tell Hilary Dwyer that her mother was about to be taken to hospital. However, Adam's words preyed on her mind for the rest of the morning. For some reason she hadn't thought any further than what would happen if she managed to find him. That had been her only concern, convincing him that he should be tested to see if he was a suitable donor.

Now she had to accept that Adam was going to be part of Hannah's life and, by default, part of hers, too. It gave her an odd feeling to know that their futures were going to be linked from now on.

Surgery came to an end at last and Beth hurried up so that she could go to the hospital in her lunch-break. Eileen was in the office when she took the notes through for filing and she couldn't help noticing that the older woman appeared to be upset.

'Are you all right, Eileen?' she asked, dropping the folders into the filing tray.

'Fine,' Eileen replied quickly. However, Beth could tell that she was anything but fine.

'You don't look it. Has one of the patients said something to upset you?' she queried, although Eileen was always so pleasant to the patients that she couldn't imagine why anyone would want to be rude to her.

'No. It wasn't a patient. It was Dr Andrews, if you really want to know.' Eileen plucked a tissue from the box on her desk and blew her nose. 'He was horrible to me just now, told me that I was inefficient because I hadn't put a lab report into a patient's file. It only arrived in the second post, and the patient had already been in to see him by then, but he wouldn't listen when I tried to explain.'

Beth frowned because it didn't sound the sort of thing Chris would normally do. She'd always found him very easy to work with and couldn't understand why he had taken Eileen to task without letting her explain what had happened.

'Do you want me to have a word with him?' she offered, but Eileen shook her head.

'No, it's all right. I appreciate it, but there's no point making a mountain out of a molehill, is there?'

She gave Beth a resigned smile as she went to fetch her coat then paused by the door. 'Oh, before I forget, Adam asked me to tell you that he is doing the home visits today.'

'Oh, right. Thanks.' Beth smiled at the older woman even though she couldn't help wondering why Adam had bothered to pass on the message.

She sighed. Of course he'd wanted her to know that he wouldn't be going with her to visit Hannah at lunchtime. She had to get used to the idea that he would want to spend as much time as possible with the little girl. Funnily enough, the thought that he would, perforce, need to spend a lot of time with her as well wasn't unpleasant.

Hannah was having her lunch when Beth arrived at the ward so she decided not to interrupt her. She went to the office instead to see if she could arrange to speak to Charles Guest, the consultant in charge of Hannah's treatment. Rose was on duty again that day and she grinned when Beth tapped on the door.

'You're a dark horse, Bethany Campbell. You didn't even *hint* that there was a new man in your life. Not that I blame you. If I had a gorgeous hunk like Adam Knight at my beck and call, I certainly wouldn't give anyone the chance to muscle in!'

Beth sighed as she perched on the edge of the desk. 'Your trouble is that you need to get out more. You should get yourself a life instead of living in that little fantasy world of yours.'

'Oh, I agree!' Rose replied cheerfully, not at all abashed. 'I'm only waiting for the right man to come along and whisk me off into the sunset. Anyway, enough about me. I want to hear all about the gorgeous, sexy Adam. You don't get many guys who are willing to give up their time to visit a sick child so he's either a saint or completely smitten with you.'

'Wrong!' Beth declared, trying to stem the tide of warmth that flowed through her veins at the thought of Adam being smitten with her.

She determinedly rid herself of such foolish notions, realising that she may as well tell Rose the truth. Rose was bound to find out who Adam was once it became common knowledge that he was being tested as a possible donor for Hannah.

'Adam Knight is Hannah's father. He's agreed to be tested to see if he can donate bone marrow to her.'

'Oh, wow! Really? Why that's just great.' Rose jumped

up and came round the desk to hug her. 'You must be so relieved, Beth.'

'Ye-es.' She shrugged when Rose stared at her in surprise. 'Of course I'm pleased that there's a possibility that he might be suitable as a donor. But I'm not sure if I did the right thing by contacting him.'

'Why ever not?' Rose demanded.

'Oh, because I promised Claire that I would never tell him about Hannah,' she explained, knowing that it was only part of the reason. The fact that Adam seemed to have such a strange effect on her wasn't something she intended to discuss with anyone, not even Rose, whom she counted as her best friend.

'I don't suppose that Claire ever imagined anything like this would happen when she made you promise,' Rose assured her after Beth had finished telling her the whole story. 'She would have wanted you to do everything you could to help Hannah.'

'I suppose so. But Adam said that he wants to be part of Hannah's life from now on—'

'Well, that's no bad thing,' Rose cut in briskly. 'At least you'll have someone to share the responsibility with. I know you love Hannah but it will make your life a whole lot easier. I mean, look at what happened between you and Ian. Would you two have split up if you'd not had all the worry of looking after Hannah to contend with?'

The phone rang at that point so Rose excused herself. Beth mouthed that she would be back later and went into the ward. Rose meant well but she didn't know the full story behind her decision to leave Ian.

She was halfway down the ward when it struck her that it no longer hurt to think about her broken engagement. It felt like something that had happened in the distant past and was no longer of any real consequence. She tried to pinpoint when everything had changed and felt her heart quicken as she realised that it had been when Adam had shown her once and for all the type of man Ian Patterson was.

Her heart gave another little jolt. Funny how everything that happened seemed to lead her right back to Adam.

Adam was already at the hospital when Beth went back to see Hannah that night after evening surgery. She'd been delayed by a patient who had arrived late then had needed a longer appointment than she'd anticipated. Adam had already left by the time she'd finished, although Chris had been still in his room.

Beth frowned as she recalled the conversation she'd had with Chris. He'd seemed extremely tense as they'd exchanged a few words about how busy the surgery had been. She couldn't shake off the feeling that there was something wrong with him.

A burst of laughter greeted her as she entered the ward. Beth frowned when she saw a group of children clustered around Hannah's bed. There were a number of parents standing on the fringes of the crowd and they were all smiling as well. However, it wasn't until she got closer that she saw what was causing all the amusement.

Adam was holding an impromptu puppet show. He had drawn a face on the side of his clenched fist with some of Hannah's crayons and draped his handkerchief over his hand to form a kind of headdress for the puppet. He was chattering away in a high-pitched voice which had reduced the children to fits of laughter.

Beth found herself smiling as well as she watched him play out a little scene that involved all of the children who were crowded around the bed. They were all enthralled by 'Nursie', the hand puppet, and eagerly responded to her questions about whether they had green spots on their tongues. It was a delightful bit of nonsense and she couldn't help thinking how much better they all looked for having such fun.

Adam suddenly spotted her and grinned wickedly. 'Aha, it's Aunty Beth,' he declared in his puppet voice. 'I wonder if *she's* got green spots on her tongue. Stick out your tongue, Aunty Beth, so that we can see.'

Beth chuckled as she poked out her tongue at him, seeing the laughter in his eyes as she complied with his instructions. It was obvious that he was enjoying himself as much as the children were and she couldn't help thinking how rare it was for an adult not to worry about making a fool of himself. Adam was comfortable with his role in life. He didn't see any need to try to impress other people yet, perversely, he did so. She only had to look at the smiling faces of the parents to realise that and her heart swelled with something which felt very much like pride.

The puppet show continued for a few more minutes before Adam announced that Nursie had to go to another ward to find the people with green spots on their tongues. There was a chorus of groans from the children but they soon cheered up when he promised that the puppet would return at a later date.

Rose started chivvying everyone back to their beds and winked at Beth as she was passing. 'Gorgeous, sexy, caring *and* fun. You lucky devil!'

Beth opened her mouth to protest but Rose had already moved away.

'I hope the staff didn't mind,' Adam said softly, drawing her attention back to him. She felt her heart perform that strange little manoeuvre again, a kind of backwards flip which was a medical impossibility but completely feasible as far as she was concerned.

He was wearing a soft blue chambray shirt that night and the colour was the perfect foil for his deep blue eyes. Beth couldn't help thinking how handsome he looked as he stood by the bed, smiling at her. He'd left the top two buttons of the shirt unfastened and through the gap she caught a glimpse of tanned skin and crisp black hair before she dragged her eyes away, aware that her heart was performing somersaults like a circus acrobat.

'I thought it would amuse Hannah while we were waiting for you to arrive,' he explained when she looked blankly at him. 'I never meant to cause such havoc.'

Well, havoc was one word to describe the effect he seemed to have had on her at least! Beth thought as he went away to fetch another chair. Her eyes followed him as he made his way down the ward and she frowned.

Why *had* her heart been acting so strangely just now?

Why *did* she feel so confused?

How *could* she explain the strange effect Adam Knight seemed to have on her?

'Are you cross, Aunty Beth?'

Hannah's worried little voice broke through her musings and she turned to smile at the little girl. 'No, of course not, poppet. Why did you think that?'

Hannah sighed. ''Cos you were frowning and you never, ever frown. Uncle Ian used to frown all the time and that's why I didn't like him.' She turned and looked over to where Adam was speaking to one of the nurses. 'I like Adam, though.'

And so could I, Beth thought as she hugged the little girl. I could like him a lot. And maybe that's at the root of all my problems. I certainly hadn't expected to feel like this about Adam Knight!

CHAPTER FIVE

'YOU WILL come back tomorrow, Adam? Promise?'

Beth sighed when she heard the pleading note in Hannah's voice. They had spent far more time at the hospital that night than she had planned on doing. Most of the other parents had left but Hannah had kept demanding that they stay a bit longer. It was obvious that the child had really taken to Adam and Beth couldn't help wondering whether that was a good thing. Admittedly, he seemed anxious to do all he could for the little girl, but would his interest last?

She groaned as she realised how perverse that thought was. Only that morning she had been worrying herself to death in case he was planning to take Hannah away from her. Now she was equally concerned that he might disappear from the child's life. It was proving impossible to find a balance where Adam was concerned!

'Cross my heart and hope to die,' Adam replied solemnly, making a cross over his heart. He whipped out his handkerchief and draped it over his hand. 'And Nursie promises she'll come back as well so long as you go to sleep now,' he added in a piping falsetto.

Hannah giggled. 'I like Nursie. Can she give me a kiss?'

'She'd be delighted to.' Adam bent and made extravagantly loud kissing noises as he touched the child's cheek.

'Now make Nursie give Aunty Beth a kiss,' Hannah ordered.

'Certainly.' Adam turned and 'kissed' Beth's cheek with his hand, once again making appropriate noises.

Beth shook her head, amused despite herself by his craziness. 'You're mad. Do you know that?'

'I shall take that as a compliment,' he observed loftily. 'Because I'm sure that's how it was meant.'

He stuffed his handkerchief back in his pocket then bent and kissed Hannah. Once again Beth was touched by the tenderness with which he treated the child.

'Night-night, darling,' he whispered. 'You have a lovely sleep and I'll see you tomorrow.'

'You have to kiss Aunty Beth, too,' Hannah murmured sleepily. 'She doesn't have anyone to kiss her goodnight now I'm not there.'

'Well, we can't have that,' Adam declared as he straightened. He placed a gentle kiss on Beth's cheek and to her surprise there was the same tenderness in his eyes when he looked at her. 'Everyone needs someone to kiss them goodnight.'

Beth summoned a smile but she couldn't deny that her pulse was racing when she bent to kiss Hannah. Why had Adam looked at her like that? she wondered dizzily.

'Goodnight, sweetheart. I'll see you tomorrow,' she murmured to the child. She didn't look at Adam as they left the ward. He couldn't possibly care about her as much as he cared about Hannah, she told herself sternly. It was silly to let her imagination start running away with her.

'I spoke to Charles Guest this afternoon, by the way. He told me that you'd had a word with him at lunchtime.' Adam glanced at her as they reached the lift. Beth made a determined effort to get her thoughts back on track and keep them there.

'That's right. I expect he told you that he's going to arrange for you to be tested as a possible donor?' she explained evenly.

'He did. I'm going to have a blood test tomorrow afternoon, in fact. The sooner we find out if I'm suitable the better.'

'I don't know what we're going to do if you and Hannah

aren't compatible,' Beth said worriedly. 'It could take ages to find another donor.'

'Let's not think about that until we get the result of the blood test,' Adam said quickly. 'Isn't there a saying about not borrowing trouble?'

'It's hard not to sometimes,' she observed sadly as she stepped into the lift.

'Hey, come on! That doesn't sound like the woman who told me last night that you have to be positive.' He smiled at her and once again she felt her heart miss a beat when she saw that same expression of tenderness in his eyes. It confused her so much to see it there that it was a relief when the lift arrived at the ground floor.

She got out and quickly made her way to the exit. She didn't enjoy feeling so mixed up so it seemed wiser to bring the evening to an end as soon as possible. However, she was forced to slow down when Adam put a detaining hand on her arm.

'Don't rush off, Beth. I was wondering if you'd come and have something to eat with me if you've not got anything planned for this evening?' He shrugged when she didn't answer immediately. 'I'm worried about Chris Andrews, to be frank. He doesn't seem himself at the moment and I wanted to hear what you thought. It's not something I feel that we can discuss in the surgery.'

'He really upset Eileen today,' she admitted. 'And that's not like Chris at all.'

'Which is precisely why I wanted to speak to you.' He didn't try to press her but she could tell that he was genuinely concerned.

'All right, then. I suppose we should try to decide if there is anything we can do,' she conceded. Although the last thing she wanted was to spend more time with Adam that night, if there was a situation developing at the surgery that was going to affect them all then she had to try to help. 'Where were you thinking of going to eat?'

'I'm open to suggestions.' He suddenly grinned. 'So long as it isn't anywhere too posh. I don't think I'm dressed for one of Winton's upmarket restaurants!'

Beth laughed at that. 'I didn't think you cared one way or the other what people thought?'

'I don't normally. However, I'd hate to disgrace you.' His smile was teasing. 'So that probably narrows it down to a fast-food restaurant. Fancy a burger?'

She shuddered. 'No, thank you! How about a take-away? There's a wonderful new Thai restaurant that's opened not far from here, and you can order meals to take out. We could stop off there and buy what we want then take it back to my flat.'

'Now, that sounds like the perfect compromise,' he agreed immediately. 'You lead the way and I'll follow you in my car. OK?'

'Fine,' she agreed.

Adam's car was parked just along the row from hers so he waited for her to back out. She checked her rear-view mirror as she exited the car park and felt her heart give a nervous little flutter when she saw him following her. She took a steadying breath but it was hard to control the inner turmoil she felt.

She sighed. She'd never envisaged that finding Adam would cause all these problems!

'That was delicious!'

Adam sank back on the bench with a groan of content-ment. They'd opted to eat outside on her tiny patio. The night was beautifully warm and it had seemed a shame to waste it by sitting indoors. While Beth had gathered together plates and cutlery, Adam had carried a coffee table outside so that they'd something to put all the waxed cartons on. They had helped themselves to the delicious food, although Adam had eaten the lion's share. Now he turned and smiled at her.

'That has to be the best meal I've had in months!'

Beth laughed as she forked up the last of her Thai green curry and rice. 'Not that you're exaggerating, of course.'

Adam had kept up an undemanding conversation while they had eaten and her former nervousness had quickly disappeared. She had decided that it was the pressure that she'd been under recently which had caused her to react so strangely earlier. It had been a stressful six months and it was bound to have had an effect on her.

'I'm not, believe me. When most of your food comes out of a tin then it's a real joy to have something that's been freshly cooked.'

She frowned. 'Why have you been eating tinned food? Was there no fresh food available where you were?'

'I'm afraid not. The area I was working in has suffered years of drought. All the crops have failed for the past two years. Most of the people living there are starving,' he explained flatly. 'There isn't any fresh food available, except for what the aid agencies have been managing to fly in to the area.'

'How terrible,' she exclaimed in dismay. 'Those poor people. I imagine there was a lot of disease in the area?'

'Dysentery was the main problem. There's hardly any clean water there and dysentery is always rife in conditions like that. That, of course, leads to severe dehydration, especially in the children. I can't begin to count the number of babies who died while I was there because they became severely dehydrated.'

'It must have been awful. Why did you choose to go into aid work? It certainly isn't the easy option,' she said softly, suddenly wanting to learn more about why he had made such a decision.

'It was something I had always wanted to do. My father was in the diplomatic service so we travelled extensively when I was a child. I realised at an early age how fortunate I was compared to most of the people I saw living in the countries where Dad was posted.' He shrugged. 'It just seemed the natural conclusion to try and do something to help them.'

'So did you apply to an aid agency as soon as you qualified?' she asked curiously.

'No. I decided that I needed to get some experience first so I went to Australia and worked there for a year. The hospital I was at was sending a team out to east Africa as part of the Australian governments's overseas aid programme and I was asked to go with them. I just never went back.'

'Did the rest of the team stay out there?' she asked in surprise.

'No, everyone but me went back home after they'd done their stint.' He shrugged. 'I stayed and joined one of the aid agencies working over there. I've been with them ever since.'

'And have you never regretted your decision?' she asked, wondering if he would have continued doing that type of work if there had been someone waiting at home for him, like Claire for instance. 'You could have been quite high up the professional ladder by now if you hadn't decided to keep doing aid work.'

'No, I've never regretted it. Until very recently I was perfectly happy with my life.'

His tone was reflective and she frowned because she wasn't sure what he meant. However, before she could work it out, he changed the subject. 'What about you, Beth? Have you ever wanted to travel or are you a home-body?'

'Oh, the latter, definitely!' She laughed when she saw his surprise. 'Sorry, but I'm not like you, Adam. I'm not at all adventurous. I've never even been tempted to work in another part of the country because I love this area so much. That must sound incredibly boring to you.'

'No, of course it doesn't. It's nice to meet someone who's

happy with her lot,' he replied with a smile. 'I take it that
Patterson felt the same way?'

'Not really. Ian is very ambitious and I imagine he'd be
happy to move around if it meant furthering his career,' she
explained with a shrug. 'Maybe that should have been a
warning that we weren't suited.'

'I don't suppose the situation would have deteriorated as
it did if you hadn't had all the stress of looking after Hannah
to contend with,' he observed bluntly. 'Without that, no
doubt you two would have been planning your wedding by
now.'

Beth laughed ruefully. 'Lucky escape, then, wasn't it?'

'So you're not sorry that you and Patterson split up?'

She frowned because there was an edge in his voice that
she couldn't understand. 'Not now. Oh, I was upset at first.
I suppose I was angry *and* disappointed. Discovering that
the man you had been planning on marrying isn't who you
thought him to be does come as a shock. However, I had
Hannah to think about so that helped. Then last night you
finally showed me just what a miserable human being Ian
really is.'

'So long as you aren't still grieving for what might have
been, Beth,' he said softly, looking at her with eyes that
seemed darker even than the night sky.

She felt a shiver run through her and looked away, but
she could hear the quavery note in her voice when she spoke
and was terrified that Adam would hear it, too. 'No, I'm no
longer grieving. Ian is part of my past and that's the end of
it.'

There was a moment's silence before he cleared his throat.
'So how have you found Chris recently?' he asked, abruptly
changing the subject.

'He certainly doesn't seem to be himself,' she replied,
struggling to keep her tone even. She took a quick breath,
trying to rid herself of the feeling that something momentous

had been about to happen before Adam had changed the subject.

'He doesn't. I admit that I don't know Chris all that well but even in the short time I've been back I've had the impression that he's very uptight at the moment. That incident with Eileen this morning is a prime example.' Adam sighed. 'The Chris Andrews I remember certainly wouldn't have reacted like that.'

'Maybe it's a result of the pressure he's been under since your uncle was taken ill,' she suggested. 'I was amazed by how busy it was here when I first started. Since Dr Wright has been in hospital, it's been Chris who's borne the brunt of the extra work.'

'I have a feeling that the problem has been going on longer than that. Chris happened to let it slip that he hasn't had any time off for almost two years.'

'Really? That would certainly explain why he's so keyed up at the moment. Nobody can work under that kind of pressure for all that time without it having an effect on them,' she said worriedly.

'Exactly. To be honest, I think that Chris is in dire need of a holiday. He needs to get right away from here so that he doesn't have to think about work, otherwise I predict that he is heading for some sort of a breakdown,' Adam stated bluntly.

'I'm sure you're right but how would we manage if Chris did take time off?' she asked, trying to work out the logistics. 'That's assuming that you can persuade him, of course.'

'It won't be easy, but I think Chris is starting to realise that something needs to be done. We shall have to see what we can come up with.' He frowned as he stared at the sky and thought about that idea. A few early stars had appeared now and they looked like sequins scattered across yards upon yards of dark blue velvet.

Beth sighed as she looked up, thinking how glorious it was to be outside on a night like that. She found her gaze drifting to Adam and it hit her that part of her pleasure stemmed from having him there with her.

As though he had sensed that she was looking at him, he suddenly glanced round. Beth saw myriad expressions cross his face in rapid succession before he smiled at her.

'I'm glad we decided to eat out here rather than in some noisy restaurant. It's such a beautiful night, far too good to waste it by sitting indoors.'

'It is,' she replied quietly, although her heart seemed to be making enough noise for both of them. She took a deep breath and willed it to calm down, but Adam's nearness was having the strangest effect on her.

She turned and stared straight ahead, deeming it wiser than continuing to look at him. 'Is that the Milky Way?' she asked pointing to a cluster of stars shimmering overhead. 'I've never been able to work out which galaxy is which.'

'That's right. And that's the Plough over there. Can you see it?'

She frowned as she tried to see what he was pointing to. 'I'm not sure…'

'A little more to your left. There.' He placed his hands on her shoulders and turned her a little more to the left. 'See. There should be seven stars in all. Count them.'

Beth quickly counted the stars then gave a gasp of delight. 'Oh, yes! I can see it now.'

She turned to him in excitement and felt her heart—which had been beating so nosily just moments before—come to a dead stop when she found herself staring into his eyes. There was a moment when neither of them moved then Adam's head dipped and his mouth found hers in a kiss that seemed to rock the whole world on its axis.

He raised his head and looked at her, and Beth felt her heart start beating again. She could feel the blood flooding through her veins, filling her with heat all of a sudden.

'Maybe I shouldn't have done that but I'm not going to

apologise,' he said softly, his deep voice grating with something that made her shiver.

'I didn't ask you to,' she replied, then gasped as she realised how that must have sounded.

He gave her a slow smile. 'Then I don't have to feel guilty about doing it again.'

His head came down once more and this time the kiss was longer, even more intense than before. Beth sighed as she felt the warm pressure of his lips settling over hers. She closed her eyes yet, strangely, she could still see the glitter of stars shimmering behind her lids.

She slid her arms around his neck, feeling her nipples harden as her breasts brushed the hard, warm muscles of his chest. It shocked her that she should be so responsive to him and she tried to draw away, but Adam wouldn't let her go.

He drew her closer instead, his hands sliding down her back and leaving behind a trail of heat wherever they touched. Beth felt as though she were on fire, burning up with heat, aching with desire to have him touch her without the barrier of clothing getting in the way. Her skin felt so sensitive all of a sudden that she could feel goose-bumps breaking out all over her as his hands continued to caress her back and shoulders. When his lips teased hers apart so that his tongue could slide inside her mouth, she didn't resist. She wanted him so much—

The sound of someone banging on the surgery door was a cruel intrusion. Beth gasped as she was brought back to the present with a jolt. It took her a moment to realise what was happening and by that time Adam was on his feet.

'I'd better go and see who that is,' he said roughly, turning to hurry inside the flat.

She quickly followed him although she was struggling to comprehend what was happening. She shot a look at Adam and felt herself go cold when she realised that he didn't appear to be having the same difficulty as she was having. Why was that? she wondered sickly. Because those kisses which had been so earth-shattering to her had been nothing more than a pleasant interlude to him?

A cold chill enveloped her as she followed him down to the surgery. It wasn't nice to think that she might have made a fool of herself. Adam must have felt her response just now and she was mortified to think that he might have been amused by it.

'Hello! Is anyone there? Please…I need help!'

'Hold on.' Adam quickly unlocked the surgery door as they heard a man's voice calling frantically from outside. 'What's the problem?'

'Oh, thank heavens you're here! I saw the lights on upstairs and that's why I knocked.' The man gestured towards a car that was parked all askew by the kerb. 'It's my wife. She's having a baby and there isn't time to get her to hospital!'

Adam took charge immediately. Turning to Beth, he quickly rapped out instructions. 'We'll use your room because it's the most suitable. Can you get everything ready? There should be an obstetrics kit somewhere about the place. And get on to the emergency services and ask them to send an ambulance here pronto, will you?'

'Will do.'

She hurried away, leaving Adam to help the anxious husband fetch his wife inside. She found the obstetrics kit in the supply cupboard, added a bundle of paper sheets and towels, then hurried to her room and got everything ready. She had just finished putting through a call to the ambulance service when the others appeared, and she gasped as she recognised the woman who was being helped into the room as Elaine Graham, the young mother they had seen the previous day.

'I didn't realise it was you,' she exclaimed, hurrying forward to help as they got Elaine onto the couch.

'I'm afraid this baby has caught us on the hop,' Elaine admitted. 'I thought I'd have plenty of time to get to hospital but everything seemed to speed up—' She broke off as another contraction began.

Beth quickly helped her out of her underwear after it had eased then placed a sterile drape over her legs. Adam was at the sink, scrubbing his hands, and he looked round with a grin.

'Maybe the baby decided he wanted to be at his big brother's party tomorrow,' he suggested.

Elaine managed a smile. 'You could be right. I only hope I'm home in time for it.'

'Well, I don't think you're going to be hanging around here for very long.' Adam had taken a pair of gloves out of the box on the counter and he went to the couch and quickly examined her. 'This baby is definitely on his way and there's no stopping him now!'

Everyone laughed, which helped ease a little of the tension. Beth found a chair for Elaine's husband, Brian, and got him settled at the head of the couch. He still looked rather pale and she could see that he was shaking.

'I wasn't with Elaine when the other two were born,' he admitted. 'I didn't think I'd be able to cope.'

'It's up to you if you want to stay,' Beth assured him, 'although I'm sure your wife would be glad of your support.'

Brian Graham took hold of his wife's hand and squared his shoulders as another contraction began. 'They always say there's a first time for everything, don't they?' He winced as Elaine gripped his fingers. 'And a last!'

Beth laughed softly as she went to join Adam. It was some time since she had assisted at a birth and she couldn't help feeling a little thrill of excitement at the thought of helping this new baby into the world. Adam was monitoring the baby's heartbeat so she waited for him to finish, feeling her heart sink when she saw the concern on his face.

He drew her away from the couch so that the parents couldn't overhear what he was saying. 'The baby's heartbeat is way too fast. It seems to be in distress. How long is that ambulance going to be?'

'At least twenty minutes. Do you have any idea what could be wrong with it?'

'It's just a guess but it could be that the cord is wrapped around its neck and cutting off its oxygen supply,' he told her, moving back to the couch. He waited until Elaine's next contraction had passed before gently examining her again.

'I'm sure that's what it is,' he said, *sotto voce*, before turning to the young mother. 'Elaine, I need you to stop pushing for me. Next time you feel a contraction pant but don't push. Understand?'

'Is there something wrong?' she asked at once, her voice rising in panic.

'I think the umbilical cord might be wrapped around the baby's neck. I need to check but I don't want you pushing because it will just draw the cord even tighter. Everything is going to be fine once I get it sorted out,' he assured her.

He tried to slide his finger around the baby's neck then shook his head. 'It is the cord but I can't get at it. There just isn't enough room.'

'Let me try,' Beth offered. 'My hands are smaller than yours.'

Adam stepped aside as she quickly bent down. Tears were streaming down Elaine's face now and Brian had gone a dreadful colour. Beth bit her lip as she gently worked her the tip of her index finger under the constricting cord wrapped around the baby's neck and, with infinite care, managed to ease it over its head.

'Well done!' Adam said, giving her a hug before turning to Elaine. 'Right, all systems go now. Let's get that little fellow out of there.'

It really was all systems go after that. Five minutes later the baby made its appearance into the world. Beth chuckled when it gave a lusty scream as she wiped its face.

'Sounds as though your new daughter is pleased to be out in the big wide world at last.'

'A girl?' Brian gulped. 'But there hasn't been a girl in our family for years!'

'Well, you've got one now.' Adam lifted the squalling infant and handed her to her mother. 'Congratulations, both of you, on a beautiful daughter.'

There was something in his voice when he said that which brought Beth's eyes winging to his face, and she felt her heart ache when she saw the sadness in his eyes. Was he thinking about Hannah's birth and all that he had missed?

It was painful to realise it, equally painful to imagine how things might have turned out. If Claire had told him about their child then maybe he wouldn't have gone to work overseas, but would that have really mattered to him if he'd had Claire and Hannah to love and care for? Maybe he and Claire would have decided to stay together after all, and they might have had more children by this time.

Beth sighed. Ifs, ands and buts didn't paint a true picture but she couldn't ignore the fact that all that could have happened. It made her wonder all of a sudden why Adam had kissed her. Because it had felt right at the time? Or because she had reminded him of Claire until he had been abruptly brought to his senses by that knock on the door?

She went to find a clean towel to wrap the baby in, pausing as she looked at Adam standing by the couch. Maybe he saw her as a substitute for her sister, but that didn't explain why *she* had kissed *him*. He certainly wasn't a substitute for Ian! Why, she had never felt like that when Ian had kissed her...

Her heart rolled over.

She had never felt like that when Ian or anyone else had kissed her.

What could it mean?

CHAPTER SIX

By the time the ambulance arrived, Adam had given the baby a thorough check-up and phoned the staff at the maternity unit to let them know what had happened. Although the baby had scored a definite nine at the five-minute Apgar test, he had wanted to be sure that they were fully aware of what had happened during her birth.

Beth finished tidying up Elaine Graham for the journey to the hospital and helped her change into one of the nightgowns Elaine had packed in her overnight case. At least it helped to take her mind off all the crazy thoughts that kept running through her head.

'There. I'm sure you must feel better now,' she said with a smile, determinedly concentrating on what she was doing.

'I do.' Elaine sighed as she looked at her daughter. 'She's perfect, isn't she? Every tiny finger and toe. I love my boys to bits but I've always longed for a daughter. I just never thought I'd be that lucky.'

'You must be thrilled,' Beth said softly, smiling as she watched the baby yawning.

'I think stunned is more the word I'd use,' Brian put in wryly. 'I still can't get over the fact that first of all she's a girl and that she arrived so quickly! Thank heavens I saw the lights on upstairs otherwise I don't know what might have happened.'

'Well, everything turned out all right in the end,' Adam said lightly as he came to join them. 'I've spoken to the sister on duty at the maternity unit and she knows what has happened. I've also written everything down in this report just to make sure that there's no confusion.'

He handed Brian an envelope then smiled at Elaine.

'However, I don't for one minute imagine that there are going to be any problems.'

'It's only thanks to you two,' Elaine said gratefully. 'Megan could have died if you hadn't managed to sort everything out.'

'Don't think about that.' Adam patted her hand when he heard the tremulous note in her voice. 'She's perfectly fine, I promise, and Megan is a lovely name for her.'

He ran a gentle finger over the baby's downy cheek. Once again Beth saw an expression of sadness cross his face before he moved aside so that the ambulance crew could transfer Elaine to a trolley. She sighed as she followed the procession out of the building and stood on the pavement to wave them off. There was no escaping the fact that Adam must bitterly regret having missed so much of his own daughter's early life.

'That's it, then. Rather an exciting end to the day, wouldn't you say?' Adam turned to her as the ambulance drove away and she summoned a smile.

'It was. I didn't think working in general practice could be so exciting.'

He laughed deeply as he relocked the surgery doors then followed her back up to the flat. 'Neither did I!'

He glanced at his watch and whistled. 'I hadn't realised it was so late. I'd better be on my way and let you get to bed. I'll just carry that table back inside for you before I go.'

'Let me get those plates first,' she said, hurrying ahead of him. She stacked the dirty dishes and empty food containers onto a tray then moved out of the way so that he could carry the table back inside. He took it back into the sitting room and looked around.

'You've made it very cosy in here, Beth. It's years since I came up to the flat. Jonathan and Mary lived here at one time until she persuaded him to move out of Winton. I think she found it a bit difficult living over the shop, so to speak.

It's been used by the odd locum since then, but I can't remember the place ever looking this welcoming.'

'I wanted to make it nice for when Hannah comes home,' she explained, glancing around in satisfaction.

She hadn't been able to afford to redecorate from scratch so she'd concentrated on making everywhere look fresh and bright by painting the walls. She'd chosen a soft peach for the sitting room, which worked well with the dark green carpet that had been laid throughout the flat. A neutral cream throw concealed the rather shabby upholstery on the old sofa, whilst bold peach and turquoise cushions added splashes of vibrant colour.

'I take it that you didn't bring much of your own furniture with you when you moved in?' Adam asked, turning to her.

'I didn't have any,' she admitted. She saw his surprise and sighed. 'I got rid of my furniture when Ian and I moved into the house we'd bought. Ian said that my things didn't go with the place.'

'Did he indeed?' He sounded annoyed. 'And didn't you have any say about how the house should be decorated?'

She shrugged, feeling a little uncomfortable because it had struck her how often she had gone along with what Ian had wanted because it had been easier than causing an argument. 'Ian had very strong views on how he wanted the place to look.'

'Ian appears to have strong views on a lot of things,' he observed so drily that she laughed.

Had he done that deliberately? she wondered as she followed him out to the patio. Deliberately tried to take the edge off her embarrassment? She sensed it was so yet she couldn't understand how he had guessed how uncomfortable she'd been feeling.

'Before I forget, how would you like to go to a party on Saturday night?'

She blinked in surprise. 'A party?'

'Uh-huh. It's being thrown in my honour, too.' His grin was engaging. 'I hope you're impressed?'

'I…um…'

He chuckled wickedly when she floundered. 'I think I've just had my answer! Serves me right, too. Anyway, James and Lillian are throwing a party on Saturday to welcome me home, and I wondered if you'd come along as my partner?'

'James Dickinson, you mean?' She felt a flurry dance along her nerves as she thought about spending another evening with Adam. Would it be wise to get any more deeply involved in the circumstances, though? She couldn't afford to forget all those ifs, ands, not to mention buts, that she had thought about earlier.

'The very same. Your ex-boss and Patterson's current one.' He suddenly frowned. 'I've no idea if James has invited Patterson along. I would imagine that he's asked some of the staff from St Jude's, though. Would it be a problem for you if he had asked him?'

She shook her head emphatically. 'Not at all.'

'Great! So that means that you'll come.' He seemed to take her acceptance as a foregone conclusion now that minor problem had been ironed out. 'I can't tell you how relieved I am.'

'Relieved?' she echoed, frantically trying to come up with an excuse that didn't sound like one.

'Yes. Lillian is a real darling but she seems to think that her main role in life is to find me a good woman to settle down with. I cringe when I think of all the poor females she's trotted out over the years for my inspection. However, I shall be spared all that if I can tell her that I'm bringing someone,' he explained in a tone of great relief.

Beth felt her heart sink like a stone and pinned a smile to her mouth to compensate for it. There was no way on earth that she was going to let him see how much it had hurt to know that he had asked her purely as a diversion from Lillian Dickinson's matchmaking tactics!

'I wouldn't like to think of you suffering unnecessarily, plus I owe you a favour for squelching Ian the other night. What time does it start?'

'I'll pick you up at eight, if that's all right with you?' His smile was pleasant so Beth couldn't understand why she had the impression that he wasn't pleased about something.

She sighed as he bade her a rather abrupt goodnight. She didn't know him all that well so it was foolish to go imagining things like that. He was probably tired after the busy day they'd had, on edge because of Hannah, worried about his uncle and concerned about Chris Andrews. All in all, he had a lot to contend with at the moment and she should bear that in mind.

She went inside then stood staring through the window at the patio, remembering what had happened out there earlier that evening. Adam had kissed her and made her feel things she had never felt before. It was going to be hard to forget that but she had to try. Hannah was the one who mattered in this situation. If it hadn't been for Hannah, she would never have met Adam.

She shivered. Maybe it was silly but she simply couldn't imagine going through her life without ever having known him.

The atmosphere in the surgery the following morning was dreadful. By mid-morning Beth was feeling totally wrung out. Chris had torn another strip off Eileen because he'd had the wrong patient's notes on his desk for a consultation. He had refused to listen to the receptionist's explanation that the patients themselves had caused the confusion by going in to see him out of turn.

It had ended up with Eileen in tears in the ladies loo, swearing that she wasn't going to stay there and be spoken to like that, and Beth doing her best to calm her down. Two cups of coffee and a lot of TLC later and Eileen was back behind her desk. However, Beth knew that the situation couldn't continue like that. It was hard enough to run the busy practice when everyone was working in harmony but it would be impossible if they were all squabbling.

She had just seen a patient out when she spotted Adam coming back from the office, so she waylaid him. 'We're going to have to do something about Chris soon,' she told him without any preamble. She quickly explained what had happened and heard him sigh.

'I thought I detected a certain frost in the air when I went to collect this,' he said, glancing at the test results that had arrived by the second post. 'Eileen certainly wasn't her usual bubbly self.'

'Chris was really rude to her,' she told him worriedly. She glanced round when she heard footsteps announcing the arrival of her next patient.

'Leave it with me. I'll have a word with him after surgery finishes. It will mean that I won't be able to go to the hospital to visit Hannah so will you explain to her that I'll see her tonight?'

'Of course. I thought you were going for the blood test this afternoon, though?'

'I am, but I won't have the time to pop in to see Hannah then because I need to be back here for the chest clinic.'

He didn't say anything more because her patient had arrived. Beth showed the woman into her room, thinking to herself that Adam had taken a lot on his shoulders when he'd come back to Winton. Of course, he couldn't have known about Hannah when he'd agreed to help, but that had only added to his worries. Did he regret finding out that he had a daughter? Or was his only regret that he hadn't found out about her sooner and thus been able to spend time with both Hannah and Claire?

Beth sighed as she closed the door. Why did one question always lead to another and never to any answers?

The patient, Joan Goodwin, was a retired headmistress, who had suffered for a number of years with varicose veins.

The situation had grown so bad that Dr Wright had referred her to a specialist, who had recommended that the affected veins should be stripped.

It had been a relatively simple procedure which had involved tying off and cutting the greater saphenous vein and its branches through an incision in the groin then withdrawing the redundant veins via a small incision in the ankle. Joan's legs had needed to remain bandaged for several weeks after the operation, so arrangements had been made for her to visit the surgery to have the bandages changed.

'So how have you been since the operation?' Beth asked, deftly removing the old bandages and popping them into a medical waste sack.

'Miles better,' Joan replied immediately. 'I was so fed up with my legs constantly aching, not to mention the fact that my feet kept swelling all the time. There is only so much time you can spend with your feet up before it drives you completely crazy!'

Beth smiled sympathetically as she began rebandaging Joan's left leg. 'I can imagine how tiresome it must have been.'

'It was. I joined a ramblers' group when I retired—there's nothing better than being out in the open country after years spent breathing in chalk dust. But for the past six months I've not been able to join them because of the problems with my veins.' Joan smiled happily. 'I'm really looking forward to the summer now. We have a number of interesting walks planned, and I'll be able to go along.'

'That's great. Right, that's all finished. You should be fine until your hospital appointment, but be sure to phone the surgery if you have any problems, won't you?' she told her, standing up.

'I shall. By the way, was that Dr Wright's nephew I saw just now as I was coming in?' Joan asked as she picked up her handbag.

'That's right. Dr Knight has very kindly agreed to step into the breach while his uncle is in hospital.'

'Now, why doesn't that surprise me?' Joan Goodwin laughed. 'Such a fine young man. I've known him for years, you see. He used to spend a lot of time here when he was younger and he was always the same—kind and considerate. His uncle told me about Adam's work and I have to take off my hat to him. You wouldn't get many young men with Adam's talent willing to do the kind of work he does.'

'No, you wouldn't,' Beth agreed warmly. She sighed as Joan Goodwin left, realising that the older woman had simply endorsed her own view of Adam. He *was* kind and caring, and dedicated and…and all manner of other things as well.

She frowned as she found herself wondering why Claire had ignored all that. Surely it must have been apparent to her sister the sort of man that Adam was? It made it even more difficult to understand why Claire had never attempted to contact him again after that first failed attempt. Unless she'd been afraid that Adam would want to pick up where they had left off?

Claire must have known that Adam was in love with her and had realised that she could never reciprocate his feelings. That had been why she'd decided that it was for the best never to seek him out and why she had made Beth promise not to do so. Claire hadn't wanted to break Adam's heart a second time.

The realisation made Beth gasp in dismay and Eileen, who happened to be passing along the corridor at that moment, must have heard her. 'Are you all right, love?' she asked, popping her head round the door.

'Um, yes, fine, thanks. Just a bit of a tickle in my throat, that's all.' Beth cleared her throat to add more weight to the small white lie but she could feel her heart aching in the strangest way. It was an effort to hide how upset she felt from the other woman. 'How are you feeling now, anyway?'

'A bit better, although I'm still annoyed about what happened.' Eileen sniffed her disapproval but Beth was pleased to see that she had been successfully distracted. 'I don't take kindly to being treated like that.'

Eileen went on her way and Beth buzzed for her next patient. However, all morning long she couldn't stop thinking about Claire and Adam, and how he might still be in love with her sister even after all this time. The strange thing was how much it hurt to think about it.

The rest of the day flew past. Beth had a free afternoon so she spent it with Hannah, reading to her and playing board games. She got back to the flat just before four after doing some shopping on the way home and was surprised to discover that Adam's car was still in the car park. She put her shopping away then went down to the surgery and tapped on his door.

'Hi, what are you doing here? Did the chest clinic drag on?'

He tossed his pen onto the desk. 'No, there were only four people booked in and they were all doing fine. It's been a while since I dealt with any asthma cases so it was interesting to bring myself up to date on the latest drug regimes.'

'The curse of the western world,' she observed. 'The latest theory is that more people are suffering from asthma because we're too clean. We're eliminating too many bugs so that we no longer have the same resistance to the allergens that provoke an asthma attack.'

'It certainly isn't as big a problem in Third World countries,' he agreed, although she couldn't help noticing that he seemed rather distracted. Her heart turned over when she suddenly remembered that he'd had to go for the blood tests that afternoon.

'It wasn't bad news, was it?'

'Sorry?' He frowned at her.

'You went for the blood tests this afternoon. I just wondered what you'd been told.'

'Nothing. I won't get to know if I'm suitable as a donor
for a few days yet.' He let out in a heavy sigh. 'I had a long
talk with Chris after surgery this morning. He's admitted that
he needs a complete break away from here.'

'I see. So what are you going to do?' she asked worriedly.

'I've already done it. I've been in touch with a couple of
agencies about hiring a locum. They've promised to fax me
a list of everyone who's available later today.'

'You aren't wasting any time. Have you talked it over
with your uncle?'

'No, nor do I intend to. I've spoken to Aunt Mary and
she agrees that it would be silly to let Jonathan know what's
happening because he will only worry.' He shrugged. 'And
the sooner I get something sorted out the better. Chris desperately needs to take some time off.'

'Well, I can't argue with that. Let's hope that you find
someone suitable quickly.' She paused but there was no way
to avoid what had to be said when it had been at the back
of her mind all day. 'You must be sorry that you came back
here. It's been one problem after another ever since you
arrived.'

'I'm not sorry that I found out about Hannah, even though
I wish that the situation had been rather different.' He looked
up and there was the oddest light in his eyes as they centred
on her. 'Coming back to Winton has changed my life, Beth.
Nothing is going to be the same as it was before.'

She wasn't sure what he had meant by that. Obviously
finding out about Hannah was bound to have repercussions
for him in the future yet she sensed there had been something else behind that statement. However, before she could
work it out, he got up.

'I'm going to make myself a cup of coffee. Do you want
one? I could do with a bit of a booster before the next round
of patients arrives.'

'Please. I spent the afternoon reading to Hannah and I feel a bit parched,' she confessed, following him to the staff-room. 'She was asking about you, by the way. I told her that you would go to see her tonight. I hope that was OK?'

Adam's face softened as he turned from plugging in the kettle. 'Of course. She's such a great little kid. It would be hard enough for an adult to cope with what she's been through in the past year.'

'She's very brave,' Beth agreed softly. 'Let's just keep our fingers crossed that the blood test results are favourable.'

'Amen to that.' He made the drinks then took them to the table and sat down. 'I think this is the worst time. Once we know one way or the other whether I'm a suitable donor then we can make plans, but everything seems rather up in the air at the moment.'

'What sort of plans?' she asked immediately.

'For Hannah's future, of course.' He put his cup on the table with a small thud that made her jump. 'I mean to be involved in her care from now on, Beth. I want you to understand that.'

'Of course. But the fact that you are out of the country for so much of the time obviously means that your time with Hannah is going to be limited.' She paused but there was no way to avoid what she had to say. 'I don't want you raising Hannah's hopes then disappointing her, Adam. It wouldn't be fair.'

'I have no intention of doing that.' He took a sip of his coffee then looked steadily at her. 'I intend to be here for Hannah for however long she needs me. It's the least I can do in the circumstances.'

'It wasn't your fault that you didn't know about her,' she said quickly, then wondered if that had been the right thing to say.

'Maybe not, but that doesn't alter the fact that I don't intend to run away from my responsibilities.' He shrugged. 'Uncle Jonathan would like nothing better than for me to work here at the surgery with him. I've always refused in the past but it could be the answer to a lot of problems.'

'You mean that you would give up your aid work?' She could hear the astonishment in her voice. She felt a little tingle run through her as the idea that Adam might be staying in Winton sank in. For some reason she felt extraordinarily pleased about it.

'Yes. I think it's time that I reassessed my life and what I intend to do in the future.'

'But are you sure that you won't regret it?' she queried, feeling that she had to play devil's advocate for herself as well as him. 'I know how important your work is to you, Adam. It won't be easy to give it up.'

'It won't. I love the work that I do because I feel that I really make a difference to people's lives. But there is no reason why I can't gain equal satisfaction from working in this country.' He must have seen her scepticism because he sighed softly.

'I know it won't be the same, Beth. But I also know that I would never forgive myself for not being here with Hannah. Why are you so surprised? Did you honestly believe that I would walk away after finding out that I had a daughter?'

'I don't think I even thought about it,' she confessed, sensing that she had hurt him.

'Then I suggest that you think about it now because it means that you and I will need to come to some sort of arrangement.' He shrugged when she looked blankly at him. 'Hannah needs you, Beth, and I accept that. But I'm hoping that in time she will come to need me, too.'

He laid his hand over hers and it seemed to her that his voice had grown deeper all of a sudden. 'Think you can put up with having me around on a long-term basis?'

'I…' Beth could hear the words she wanted to say echoing inside her head, a polite little speech which wouldn't cause offence. The problem was that she couldn't seem to get them out into the open. It was the way that Adam was looking at her, she decided dizzily. As though her answer really *mattered* to him.

'I suppose so,' she managed at last then flushed when he laughed.

'You could have tried to inject a *bit* more enthusiasm into your voice.' He sobered abruptly. 'I do understand your concerns, though, Beth. Really.'

'Do you?' she asked, wishing that he would explain them to her. Why did she always end up feeling so confused? She had prided herself on being able to cope with most situations yet dealing with Adam seemed to be the one exception.

'Yes. It's what you said, about me going away after Hannah has grown fond of me.' He gave her hand a final squeeze then let it go. 'I won't let her down. I promise you. I'm here to stay, Beth. You can be sure of that.'

He picked up his cup and stood. 'Now I think I'll go and see if that fax has arrived. The sooner we find ourselves a locum, the sooner Chris can take that holiday.'

Beth sighed as he left the room. Maybe that would solve one particular problem but there were so many others. Whilst she didn't doubt that he was sincere about wanting to be here for Hannah, she wasn't convinced that it was the right thing for him to do.

Could he really settle down to the life of a rural GP after what he had been used to? Adam had just admitted that he had refused to consider working at the surgery in the past, so was it right for him to decide to do so now out of a sense of duty? She couldn't bear to think that he might grow to resent Hannah, and maybe come to blame *her* for involving him in the little girl's life.

People always said that you should follow your heart, but where did Adam's heart really lie? Here in this small Cheshire town or thousands of miles away in a different continent?

CHAPTER SEVEN

THE NEXT two days flew past. Between working and visiting Hannah, Beth had hardly any time for herself. Fortunately, Chris had cheered up and the atmosphere in the surgery had improved dramatically after he had apologised to Eileen. Obviously the thought of his forthcoming break had made a world of difference to him. By the time Saturday rolled around, everyone was feeling much better.

It was emergencies only at Saturday morning surgery so Beth didn't have to work. She took the opportunity to go into town to look for something to wear for the party that night. She'd not bought herself anything new for ages and the thought of having to dig out one of her faithful old stand-bys for the occasion certainly didn't appeal. No matter why Adam had seen fit to invite her, she intended to look her best.

She finally found the perfect dress in a small boutique off the high street. It was a wonderful shade of jade green which made her fine skin look like porcelain and emphasised the richness of her red-gold hair. Its simple lines made the most of her slim figure whilst the knee-length skirt showed off her shapely legs to full advantage.

Beth took a deep breath and said she would have it, refusing to think about the extremely large hole it was going to make in her meagre savings. It looked wonderful on her and it had been ages since she had treated herself.

She paid Hannah an early visit that evening, wanting to give herself enough time to get ready for the party. She was just about to leave when Adam arrived, although she almost didn't recognise him. Her mouth fell open as she took stock of the smart navy trousers he was wearing with a creamy-coloured shirt and highly polished black shoes. He'd even had his hair cut and the crisp black waves were now neatly brushed back with just one unruly strand falling over his forehead.

'I think Aunty Beth is impressed.' He winked at Hannah, who giggled. 'Either that or she's catching flies.'

Beth closed her mouth with a snap. 'I *am* impressed. I hardly recognised you, in fact. Are you sure that you're really Adam Knight?'

'I think so.' He gave her a wide smile as he half turned. 'Want to check if I've got a name tape sewn into the back of my shirt then you'll know for certain?'

She laughed. 'No, thank you very much! I shall take your word for it.'

'He really is Adam,' Hannah put in worriedly. 'I'm sure he is, Aunty Beth.'

'There, you've no need to worry. Hannah knows who I am even if you have your doubts.' Adam's tone was light enough yet Beth felt a ripple run through her. She frowned as she watched him bend down to look at something Hannah wanted to show him. Had she imagined that strange undercurrent in his voice just now?

She shrugged aside the feeling, knowing that it was pointless going down that route again. Whenever she started wondering what Adam was thinking she ended up feeling even more confused.

'I'd better be off, then, if I don't want you to outshine me at this party,' she said lightly, bending to kiss Hannah. 'I'll see you tomorrow morning, sweetheart. OK?'

'Will you tell me all about the party?' Hannah pleaded.

'Of course I will.' Beth gave the child a last hug then straightened.

'I'll pick you up around eight,' Adam told her, taking her place by the bed.

'Would you like me to drive?' she suggested. 'After all,

this party is being held in your honour so you may as well enjoy it.'

'I don't need to have a drink to enjoy myself,' he told her with a grin. 'Not to mention that my mother would have had a pink fit if she'd found out I'd allowed a lady to chauffeur me around. She was a stickler for good manners.'

'Well, I would hate to ruin all her good work so I'll expect you at eight, then.'

Beth gave him a smile then hurried away. She paused to glance back and felt her heart lift when she saw them huddled together. Hannah was laughing at something Adam had said to her and her face was glowing with happiness. Suddenly she was convinced that she had made the right decision by contacting Adam, despite any problems that might arise in the future.

She left the ward, refusing to dwell on how that decision was going to affect her. It was Hannah who mattered most.

Beth had just finished getting ready when Adam arrived spot on eight o'clock. She shot a last satisfied glance in the mirror then hurried to the door, secure in the knowledge that she had been right about the dress. It had been ages since she had taken so much trouble getting ready but she knew that she looked her best.

He gave an appreciative whistle when he saw her. 'Wow! What can I say except that you look stunning.'

'Thank you kindly, sir!' Beth smiled at him, feeling a small glow of happiness inside her when she saw the warmth in his eyes. 'You don't look so bad yourself, as I think I mentioned earlier.'

'I decided that I should make an effort for once so I went into town this morning.' He grimaced. 'It's been so long since I bought myself any new clothes that I couldn't remember what size I take! Fortunately, the guy in the shop helped me out.'

'Well, one of you certainly has good taste,' she assured

him as she locked the door. 'Have you tracked down your luggage yet, by the way?'

'Last reported sighting, it was languishing in Milan,' he informed her, opening the car door with a flourish. 'Your carriage awaits you, madam!'

'Thank you, James,' she said in a suitably regal tone. She waited until he had got into the driver's side before continuing, 'How did your bags get to Milan? It wasn't on your route, was it?'

'Nope.' Adam started the engine and drove out of the surgery car park. 'The airline has no idea how they got there. It's one of those little mysteries that are destined never to be solved. However, they assured me that they will have my cases ready and waiting for me at Manchester airport in the morning.'

'That's something, I suppose. But it must have been very inconvenient for you. I imagine you could claim some kind of compensation?' she suggested.

'I don't think having a couple of suitcases go missing is all that high up the scale of earth-shattering events,' he said easily. 'It's just one of those things.'

'Not many people would agree with you there. I remember Ian taking me to Paris not long after we started going out together and making a huge fuss because his case had been damaged in transit.'

'I find it hard to worry about things like that. They just don't seem important. It's people who matter, not things.' He grinned wickedly. 'Anyway, if you saw the state of my clothes then you'd know why I wasn't unduly worried if my bags *never* turned up!'

Beth laughed but she knew that what he'd said had made an impression on her. Adam was so different to the other men she had known. Granted, she'd not had all that many boyfriends and no real relationships until she'd met Ian, but Adam stood out. He cared about the things that really mattered in life and didn't waste time on incidentals.

Maybe it was as a result of the life he had led yet she didn't fully believe that. It was an intrinsic part of his nature and she found it very appealing, but, then, there were a lot of things about him which appealed to her.

The thought stayed with her throughout the drive to James and Lillian Dickinson's house. Beth couldn't deny that she found it worrying that she liked him so much. In the end, she decided that it might be better not to dwell on it and focused on the forthcoming party. It was obvious that James and Lillian intended to give Adam a warm welcome home from the number of cars parked in the driveway of their large detached house.

Lillian met them at the door, smiling in delight when she saw Beth. 'Beth! Oh, how lovely to see you. Adam never told us he was bringing you along tonight.'

'I thought it would be a nice surprise for you.' Adam laughed as he bent and kissed Lillian's cheek. 'You're looking well. I think blooming is the word.'

Lillian chuckled as she smoothed her elegant navy maternity gown over her stomach. 'I haven't felt as though I was *blooming*, I assure you! I was horribly sick for the first three months but things have got a bit better of late.'

'Isn't this your third baby?' Beth asked, following her inside.

'Third *and* fourth!' Lillian laughed when she saw her surprise. 'That's right, *it* is *them*. We're having twins.'

'Congratulations!' Adam hugged her then turned as James came out of the sitting room to greet them. 'Lillian was just telling us your news. You kept that very quiet when I spoke to you the other day.'

James laughed good-naturedly as he looped an arm around his wife's shoulders. 'I thought it might sound as if I was bragging. Anyway, if you got your act together, Adam, it could be your turn to enjoy all those sleepless nights in the not-too-distant future.'

Beth shifted uncomfortably when she saw a shadow cross

Adam's face before he made some light rejoinder. They moved into the sitting room and Lillian took her away to be introduced to anyone she hadn't met. Fortunately, there were a lot of people there from St Jude's so she didn't feel out of place. Adam was talking to a group of James's friends, and he appeared to be happy enough. However, Beth knew that the remark had touched a chord by reminding him how much he had missed of Hannah's first few years of life. The fact that the little girl's future hung in the balance must simply add to his pain.

Conversation flowed throughout the evening. Beth was kept busy at one end of the room and Adam always seemed to be talking to someone at the other. They finally met up again when Lillian announced that supper was served in the dining room. Adam nipped smartly into the queue by the buffet table and smiled at her.

'You were saving me a place, I hope?' he teased, grinning when a couple of people behind started catcalling about queue-jumpers.

'So it appears,' she agreed with heavy irony.

He wasn't the least abashed. 'I *am* supposed to be the guest of honour.'

'Only because James couldn't think of a better excuse to throw a party.'

'Ouch, that hurt!' He clutched a hand to his heart. 'You'd think I'd know by now not to go expecting compliments from you, Beth. You shoot from the hip, as the Americans say.'

They reached the buffet table just then and he handed her a plate. Picking up a napkin-wrapped bundle of silverware, he studied it consideringly. 'I wonder if it's safe to let you loose with this. I don't fancy a knife between the ribs.'

'Guns and knives indeed. You've obviously been mixing with the wrong sort of people,' she declared loftily, filling her plate with some of the delicious food on offer. Lillian must have pulled out all the stops because the table was groaning under an array of delicacies guaranteed to tempt even the most discerning palate.

'Which is why it's probably a good job I'm back in Winton.' He grinned as he piled slices of delicious looking roast beef onto his plate. 'You can save me from going any further down the road to ruin.'

'Oh, you can rely on Beth to keep you on the straight and narrow,' James put in from where he was standing behind the table, playing the genial host. 'She kept us all in order when she was on the coronary care unit. She was the best sister I've ever worked with. I pray every day that she'll change her mind and come back to us.'

'Hands off! You're not poaching her back, Dickinson. I need her at the surgery,' Adam warned him, laughing.

'Maybe not *just* at the surgery either,' Lillian chipped in, smiling pointedly at him.

Adam laughed. '"No comment" is the phrase, I believe.'

He passed off the moment in his usual easygoing manner, without betraying a hint of discomfort. How Beth wished that she could treat it so casually, but her heart was thumping like crazy.

She picked up the pepper pot and abstractedly sprinkled the condiment onto her plate. There were all sorts of reasons why Adam *needed* her, ranging from the work she did at the surgery to taking care of Hannah. However, all of a sudden none of them seemed to be quite sufficient. How lovely it would be if he needed her simply for herself.

The thought slid into her mind with such lightning speed that she gasped. Adam looked curiously at her. 'Are you OK?'

'I think a bit of pepper must have gone up my nose,' she explained hastily, putting the pepper pot back on the table.

'No wonder.' His brows rose as he looked pointedly at her plate. Beth blushed when she saw the liberal amount of black pepper that she had sprinkled over her food.

'I...um...love pepper,' she said lamely, then quickly

changed the subject. 'Shall we sit down? We're holding up the queue.'

'Sure.' Adam didn't say anything more as she led the way across the room, but she could see the tiny smile that had curled the corners of his mouth and knew that he hadn't believed her explanation. The one comforting thought was that he couldn't possibly have guessed what had been going through her mind.

She sighed as they sat down. She had to get a grip on herself. Her main concern at the moment had to be Hannah. How she felt about Adam had to take second place to her niece's welfare.

'This is delicious, almost as good as that take-away we had the other night.' Adam smiled at her. 'Let's hope that this evening doesn't come to quite such an exciting end, though.'

Beth returned his smile, relieved to settle on such a safe topic. 'Did I tell you that Brian phoned to thank us for what we did? He said that Elaine and the baby were both fine, although the consultant had decided to keep them in hospital for a couple of days just to be on the safe side.'

'So she didn't make it to her son's birthday party after all?'

'I'm afraid not. Brian had to organise it by himself.' Beth laughed as she recalled their conversation. 'He told me that it was harder sorting out a group of under-fives to play musical chairs than it was finalising a multi-million-pound deal!'

'I can imagine,' he agreed ruefully, then suddenly sighed. 'I have a lot to learn about looking after children. I know how to care for the ones who are sick, although it's different when it's your own child who is ill, I have to say. But it's the everyday things which I have no experience of, all those little things that you need to do to make sure they're safe and happy.'

'It isn't that difficult,' she said quietly. 'You'll learn if you really want to.'

'You still have doubts, don't you, Beth? You don't really believe that I mean it when I say that I intend to be here for Hannah?'

His voice had hardened, hinting that he was annoyed that she seemed to doubt his sincerity. Even though she didn't want to promote an argument Beth, knew it would be wrong to dismiss her concerns.

'I admit that you've settled into the job at the surgery seemingly without any problems, but it's early days yet, Adam.'

'And I might regret my decision in the future?' He stared at the floor. 'I won't lie to you and claim that it will be easy. It *is* a big step to take but I'm sure that it's the right thing to do for a number of reasons. You'll just have to trust me on this, Beth.'

She sighed when she heard the edge in his voice. 'I'm sorry if it seems as if I don't believe you. But my main concern is that Hannah doesn't get hurt in the future—that, plus whether you'll be able to donate bone marrow to her, of course.' Her voice quavered because the thought was so difficult to deal with. 'If she doesn't get this transplant, she might not have a future to worry about.'

'Don't! I can't bear to imagine anything happening to her.' His expression was bleak. 'I couldn't stand to lose her when I've only just found her.'

'Sorry.' Beth glanced at him. 'It must have been a shock when you discovered that you had a daughter, though.'

'It still is. I wake up each morning and find myself wondering if I've dreamt it.' His smile was tinged with sadness. 'I wish I'd dreamt part of it anyway, the bit about her being ill.'

'If only you'd seen her last year,' she began, then broke off. 'Sorry again. That was a crass thing to say in the circumstances.'

'I'd give anything to have known about her sooner but I can't turn back the clock. Those years are gone so I have to focus on the future.'

'Did you never wonder if I was telling you the truth about Hannah?' she asked curiously. 'I mean, I just confronted you with the fact that she was your child and you seemed to accept it without question.'

'No one would lie about a thing like that, especially not in the circumstances,' he said bluntly. 'Anyway, I only had to see that photograph of her to know who she was. Hannah looked exactly like my sister, Sarah, at the same age.'

'I didn't know that you had a sister,' she exclaimed.

'She died when she was ten. She had a congenital heart problem and was always delicate.' His smile was sad. 'Sarah was seven years younger than me so I was very much the big brother figure to her. Her death hit me hard. It was that which made me decide to go into medicine. I wanted to help save the lives of children like Sarah.'

'I had no idea. Claire never told me anything about your background. I wish she had, though.'

'I wish she had, too. Things might have turned out very differently for all of us.'

He didn't say anything else because one of James's friends came over to speak to him just then. Beth gathered together their plates, wondering what he had meant by that last remark. She sighed as she took the plates through to the kitchen, where Lillian was loading the dishwasher. He had probably meant that he would have got to know about Hannah sooner, but would she have contacted him after Claire died if the child hadn't been taken ill?

It was strange to think that everything that had happened in the past six months hinged on her niece's illness. If just one link in that chain of events had been broken she might never have met Adam. The thought made her shiver as though the spectre of something dreadful had walked over her grave.

'Has Adam been commandeered by someone else after a vicarious thrill?' Lillian asked with a grin as Beth handed her the dirty plates. 'Everyone wants to hear about his aid work, even though none of us could face the kind of life he leads,' she explained when Beth looked blankly at her.

'I know I couldn't,' she agreed, struggling to shake off the awful thought that their paths might never have crossed.

'That could cause problems, I imagine?' Lillian observed, looking quizzically at her.

'Problems?' Beth flushed when she realised what the other woman was getting at. 'Oh, Adam and I aren't involved that way.'

'No? Then which way are you *involved*?' Lillian laughed. 'Come on, Beth, confess! Adam is gorgeous. I defy any woman to remain immune to his charms. If I wasn't so happily married—and decidedly pregnant—I would succumb myself.'

'It isn't what you think, Lillian—honestly. Adam is Hannah's father. I'd been trying to find him for ages when he suddenly turned up at the surgery where I work. I had no idea that he was Dr Wright's nephew.'

'Hannah's father? Really?' Lillian was obviously stunned by the news. Beth quickly filled her in on the details then shrugged.

'So you can see that the situation isn't quite what you thought it to be. The only real link that Adam and I have is Hannah.'

'But you'd like it to be more than that, wouldn't you?' Lillian shook her head before Beth could say anything. 'No, you don't have to answer that. James is always telling me to stop interfering in other people's affairs. I just hope that everything works out for you and Hannah. You two deserve some happiness after the last twelve months.'

'You won't repeat what I've told you, will you?' Beth asked quickly, wondering if she should have told the other woman about Adam's relationship to Hannah without asking him first. It was something they hadn't discussed but she must do so soon.

'My lips are sealed,' Lillian began, then broke off as there was a loud crash followed by a wail of 'Mummy' from upstairs. 'Sounds as though the natives are getting restless. I'd better go and read the kids the Riot Act. I bribed them to stay out of the way with a video and two *huge* tubs of popcorn. Maybe Dr Spock wouldn't have recommended it as an example of good parenting, but it works for me!'

Beth laughed as Lillian hurried away. She turned to go back to the party then stopped when she found herself confronted by Ian Patterson. She'd heard the doorbell ringing while she'd been talking to Lillian but she hadn't realised that Ian was one of the guests who had arrived.

'Hello, Beth. I'm surprised to see you here. Did James need to boost the number of spare women, then?'

'Probably,' she replied, refusing to rise to the bait. She walked to the door but he made no attempt to get out of her way.

'What's the hurry? Surely you've got time to stay and chat? I'm sure nobody will miss you for a few minutes.'

His gaze swept over her assessingly. 'My, my, you have made an effort tonight. Maybe you should have tried harder when we were together instead of spending all your money on that kid. Then I might not have been so keen to get rid of you.'

'It was me who got rid of you, Ian. Remember?' she said sweetly. 'And I have to say that it was the best thing I ever did.'

'I wonder if you'll still feel like that in a couple of years time?' His face twisted into an ugly smile. 'I can't see many men wanting to take on someone else's child, unless you're pinning your hopes on that lout you were with the other night. I couldn't believe it when James told me he was a doctor. It's amazing the kind of person they allow into the profession nowadays.'

'It certainly is. Funny, I never thought you and I would have much in common, Patterson, but it seems that we agree on one point at least.'

Beth froze. She looked up and saw Adam standing in the doorway. That he must have heard every word that Ian had said was obvious from his expression. She felt a shiver run through her as he came into the room and smiled at the other man because it wasn't a pleasant smile by any means.

'Let's see if we agree on something else. I think you owe Beth an apology, don't you?' he said in a conversational tone that was underpinned with steel.

'I...um...I have nothing whatsoever to apologise for!' Ian blustered, going red.

'I disagree.' Adam's smile didn't waver but the tone of his voice was little short of dangerous. Obviously, Ian must have thought so, too, because he treated Beth to a look of pure loathing.

'I apologise.'

'There. That didn't hurt a bit, did it?' Adam looped his arm around her shoulders and led her to the door where he paused. 'A few words of warning. If I ever hear you speaking to Beth like that again, it won't be an apology that I'll be expecting from you.'

Beth didn't say a word until they were back in the sitting room. James had put on some music and everyone was dancing. She waited until they had reached a quiet corner then slid out from beneath Adam's arm.

'I'm so sorry that you had to overhear that,' she began, mortified that he should have witnessed such a nasty scene. She couldn't believe that Ian would have said such horrible things to her.

'Hold it right there.' He placed a gentle finger against her lips. 'It isn't your fault that your ex-fiancé has a talent for making a fool of himself. Now, let's forget all about him and get on with enjoying ourselves. How about chancing your luck and dancing with me?'

She hesitated as the music suddenly changed to an old rock and roll classic. 'I don't know how to rock and roll, I'm afraid.'

'Neither do I so we should be perfectly matched,' he declared, taking hold of her hand and leading her into the fray of gyrating couples. However, instead of trying to twirl her round he simply put his arms round her waist and began to shuffle around the floor, betraying a remarkable deftness as he steered her past all the flailing bodies.

'This is cheating!' she declared, laughing up at him.

His eyes crinkled as he smiled at her. 'I won't tell if you don't,' he said in a tone that made the music and everyone else fade into the background.

Beth felt her pulse leap as she stared into his warm blue eyes for a second longer before he drew her closer, cradling her head against his shoulder as they circled the floor. The music must have changed at least a dozen times but Adam made no attempt to follow the tempo as they moved to their own rhythm.

She caught Lillian's eye as she passed her and James dancing together, and smiled when her friend winked at her. It was obvious what was going through Lillian's mind and equally obvious what Ian was thinking when they passed him, too.

Beth averted her eyes as Ian scowled at her, not wanting anything to spoil the mood. Maybe it was silly to let herself get carried away, but what harm could there be in enjoying Adam's company?

The feeling of contentment stayed with her for the rest of the evening. They left the party shortly after midnight and Adam drove them back to her flat, keeping up an undemanding conversation about the people they had spoken to. He drew up behind the surgery and switched off the engine.

'I'll see you up to the flat,' he offered, leaning over to open her door for her.

'I could make us some coffee, if you like,' she suggested, not wanting the night to end just yet.

He smiled at her, his eyes very warm as they rested on her. 'That sounds good if you're sure it won't be any trouble.'

'Of course not!' She gave a throaty laugh, hearing the thread of excitement it held. She quickly got out of the car and hurried up the steps to the door.

Adam was just coming in for coffee, she told herself sternly. It was the least she could do after he'd invited her to the party. However, she couldn't deny that her heart was hammering when she heard him following her up the steps.

'I'll put the kettle on,' she said, going straight to plug it in.

'Where do you keep the cups?

'In the cupboard over the hob,' she replied, turning round to fetch the milk from the fridge just as he started towards the cupboard. They collided with a thud and Adam's hands shot out to steady her when she rebounded off him.

'Oops, sorry! I didn't mean to trample you into the ground in the rush!'

'That's OK,' she said shakily, feeling the tremor that snaked through her when she felt the warmth of his hands on her bare skin. The contrast between the coolness of her flesh and the warmth of his was sending ripples of awareness spiralling through her whole body.

'Are you cold?' he asked, his voice sounding very deep all of a sudden in the silence. There was only the hum of the refrigerator in the background and that was too quiet to intrude. In a funny sort of way, it felt as though they were the only two people in the whole wide world, yet it wasn't an unpleasant feeling by any means.

'Not really. It's just that your hands are so warm...'

'And your skin is so cool,' he finished for her, bending so that the last words were spoken against her lips.

His mouth was equally warm when it covered hers. Beth

shivered again and felt him smile as he drew her closer. His arms wound around her body and it was like it had felt on the dance floor, only better because this time they were alone. There was no one to see and wonder when he deepened the kiss, no one to comment when she kissed him back. This was their time and nobody else's. It made it even more special.

His lips brushed hers in one last achingly tender kiss before he sighed. 'I would love to let this continue but I think it would be a mistake, don't you, Beth?'

'Would it?' she whispered, then felt her face heat as she realised how that must have sounded.

'Yes.' He set her gently away from him and his eyes were so dark a blue that they seemed almost black at that moment. 'We don't want to do anything that we might regret. It's all too easy to do things for the wrong reasons.'

She wasn't sure what he meant by that yet couldn't bring herself to ask. Maybe Adam could rationalise away his feelings but she couldn't.

She stepped out of his arms, praying that he couldn't tell how hurt she felt. 'I expect you're right. I'll make that coffee.'

'I think I'll give it a miss after all. It's very late and I'll only end up not being able to sleep if I drink coffee at this time of the night.'

He smiled at her but his expression was guarded. 'Thanks for the offer, though, Beth.'

'You're welcome,' she replied flatly, knowing in her heart that it had been an excuse. Adam was anxious to leave because he didn't want to run the risk of there being a repeat of that kiss. But he had been the instigator of it so why had he changed his mind so abruptly?

She saw him to the door, wondering why he'd had such a rapid change of heart, but it wasn't until she was switching off the lights that an explanation occurred to her.

Had Adam kissed her in the first place because she'd reminded him of Claire, then had he had second thoughts about what he was doing? He'd said something about doing things for the wrong reasons so it seemed to fit.

Her heart was heavy as she went to her bedroom and undressed. The thought that Adam might have used her as a substitute for her sister was too painful. She didn't want to be second best!

She got into bed then lay tossing and turning as the thought played tag through her dreams. It was almost a relief when the sound of the telephone ringing roused her an hour later. However, her relief was short-lived when she discovered that it was the hospital calling to tell her that Hannah was ill.

She dragged on some clothes then hesitated, undecided whether she should ring Adam and tell him what had happened. The last thing she wanted was to have to speak to him when her thoughts were in such turmoil, but he had a right to know. She had to discount everything else and just remember that he was Hannah's father.

She picked up the phone and her heart felt like lead when it struck her that that was all he might ever be.

CHAPTER EIGHT

'How is she? What have the doctors said?'

Beth was in the waiting room when Adam arrived at the hospital some ten minutes after she had got there. She put down the cup of rather gritty coffee that she had bought from the machine in the corner and turned to him.

'It appears that she's got some kind of infection. They're doing tests at the moment to find out what it is, but that's all I know, apart from the fact that they've moved her to a side room.'

'She was fine when I left her.' Adam sank onto a hard plastic chair and ran his hands over his face. Beth could see the fear that had clouded his eyes when he looked at her beseechingly.

'You saw her yourself, Beth. There didn't seem to be anything wrong with her, did there?'

'No, but the doctor I spoke to told me that these things can happen right out of the blue. Hannah is just so susceptible at the moment because of her treatment.' She summoned a smile, hating to see him suffering like that. 'You must know that already, but I don't want you blaming yourself because you didn't suspect that she might be ill.'

'I did but thanks anyway for reminding me.'

He gave her a smile then stood up and began pacing the floor. Beth picked up her coffee then put it down again after only a few sips, unable to stomach the lukewarm liquid when her insides were churning. She glanced at her watch then looked up to find that Adam was checking his and sighed.

'It's different when you're personally involved, isn't it? I must have dealt with thousands of similar situations over the years, but you never fully appreciate what the relatives are going through until you experience it yourself.'

'I know what you mean. Part of me is trying to be strictly professional by focusing on the thought that Hannah is receiving the best care possible, but the other part… Well!' He held his hands wide open in a gesture that hinted at how helpless he felt.

'You're probably sorry that I phoned you,' she suggested softly.

He shook his head. 'I would have been upset if you hadn't called me. I meant what I said about wanting to be here for Hannah. Her welfare is my number-one priority.'

Had that been a warning? Beth wondered, watching as he strode to the window. But a warning about what exactly? That she shouldn't try to exclude him from any decisions that concerned Hannah?

It seemed the most logical explanation yet she sensed that there had been something more to that statement. She sighed as she realised that once again she was falling into the trap of trying to work out what Adam was thinking. What chance did she have of succeeding when she found it impossible to sort out the muddle inside her own head?

It was almost an hour before Neil Bartlett, the specialist registrar, appeared to update them on Hannah's condition. Beth shot to her feet as soon as she saw him coming along the corridor.

'How is she?' she demanded, hurrying to the door.

'Not too bad,' he said reassuringly as he came into the room. 'We've managed to track down the source of the infection to her catheter.'

'Really?' she exclaimed. At the start of Hannah's treatment a catheter had been inserted into a large vein near her heart. All the drugs and transfusions of blood and platelets she needed were administered via this tube. Children especially found it far less stressful to have a permanent line in place.

'At least we now know what has caused the problem, which is a step in the right direction,' Neil continued. 'It's unfortunate, but it does sometimes happen despite the most stringent nursing care. I've removed the old catheter and inserted a fresh one so, hopefully, things should start to improve from now on.'

'I take it that Hannah is being given intravenous antibiotics,' Adam put in.

'That's right. She's been having them all along as part of her treatment but I've upped the dosage. They should start to take effect within a few hours,' Neil agreed pleasantly. Beth could tell that he was curious about who Adam was so she quickly made the introductions.

'This is Hannah's father, Dr Adam Knight.'

'Nice to meet you. My boss said that you'd been to see him. He was delighted that you've agreed to be tested as a possible donor for Hannah,' Neil said enthusiastically, shaking hands. 'Anyway, I expect you want to see Hannah now so I'll take you through. She's still very feverish but she's been asking for you and for someone called Nursie as well. None of us knew who she meant, to be honest.'

Neil looked enquiringly at them as Beth laughed. 'Would you believe that Nursie is a hand puppet? Adam invented her the other night and Hannah was rather taken with her.'

'Oh, I see. That explains it, then.' Neil laughed as he led the way along the corridor. 'Now, don't worry if Hannah seems a bit spaced out. It's just because she's still very feverish.' He grimaced. 'Sorry. A bit like teaching your grandmother to suck eggs, telling you two that! Put it down to it having been a long night.'

He showed them into the room then left. Beth hurried straight to the bed, her heart turning over when she saw how ill Hannah looked. There were huge black circles under the little girl's eyes and her skin was burning hot when Beth gently stroked her thin little cheek.

'Hi, monster. What have you been up to, then? The doctor

says that you've got some nasty bugs making you feel poorly.'

Hannah's eyes were clouded with fever. 'I was sick, Aunty Beth, and my head hurts,' she whispered.

'You'll feel better soon, darling,' she assured her. She glanced round as Adam came to join her. 'Look who's here. Adam wanted to come and see how you were, sweetheart.'

'Did you bring Nursie?' Hannah murmured through parched and cracked lips.

'Nursie said to tell you that she'll be here in the morning after you've had a sleep,' he told the child gently. He stroked her hot little cheek and Beth could see that his hand was trembling. It was obvious to her, if not to Hannah, that Adam was struggling to keep control of his emotions, and her heart went out to him for what he must be suffering.

'All right.' Hannah's eyes had started to shut but they suddenly shot open again. 'Will you stay with me? Both of you?'

Adam took hold of the little girl's hand then reached for Beth's as well. 'Yes, we'll both stay. Now, you go to sleep and we'll see you in the morning, sweetheart.'

Hannah's eyes closed once more and she fell asleep almost immediately. Adam sighed as he stood by the bed and watched her. 'It breaks your heart to see her like this, doesn't it?'

'She'll be fine,' Beth assured him, hoping that she wasn't tempting fate by saying that. A shudder ran through her at the thought of what might happen if the antibiotics failed to work. There were no guarantees that they would and Hannah was so frail…

Adam gently let go of Hannah's hand so that he could turn Beth towards him. He bent and looked deep into her eyes. 'Just focus on the thought that Hannah is going to beat this. Never, ever underestimate the power of positive thought.'

She managed a wobbly smile, feeling a little better because he had sounded so confident. 'I'll try.'

'Good.' There was a moment when she thought that he was going to say something else but then he let her go. Moving to the far side of the bed, he pulled up a chair and sat down.

Beth sat down as well, focusing all her energy on willing Hannah to overcome this setback. She glanced at Adam and could tell that he was doing the same thing. In a funny kind of way it made her feel closer to him than she had felt to anyone in the whole of her life. How strange. But then her response to him had been strange from the outset, only now really wasn't the time to start wondering why.

It was a long and tiring night. There was no chance even to doze because Hannah was charted for fifteen-minute observations. Every time Beth's eyes started to close a nurse would appear to check how the little girl was doing. By the time dawn crept across the sky, she was exhausted and felt at least a hundred years old. However, the good news was that Hannah seemed to be responding to the antibiotics because her temperature had started to drop.

'Thank heavens for that,' Adam said softly as the nurse left the room after telling them the good news. He got up and stretched, groaning as he worked the kinks out of his spine. In the pale morning light his face looked grey and drawn but he still managed a smile. 'She's a real little fighter, isn't she?'

'She is.' Beth smiled back at him, feeling the relief pouring through her in a great wave. She got up as well, wincing as her legs protested after all the hours spent sitting on a hard hospital chair. 'Oh, I'm stiff as a board! What wouldn't I give for a long, hot shower.'

Adam's brows rose. 'Go and have one, then. I'll stay here in case Hannah wakes up.'

'Are you sure?' she asked hesitantly. Although she was

sorely tempted to accept his generous offer, it didn't seem
fair to leave him there while she took a break.

'Of course I'm sure. I think you can trust me not to disappear for the next half-hour.'

His tone was sharp and she sighed when she realised that
he had misunderstood her hesitation. 'I never thought that
you would. It just didn't seem fair to leave you here when
you must be as exhausted as I am.'

His voice instantly softened. 'Sorry. I didn't mean to bite
your head off. Put it down to tiredness. OK?'

She shrugged. 'Of course. But can we get one thing
straight, Adam. I don't doubt for a minute that you're sincere
about wanting to be here for Hannah.'

'But you still have doubts even after the discussion we
had last night?' he put in. 'Come on, Beth, let's not beat
about the bush. Admit it.'

'All right, then, yes.' She faced him squarely, although
her heart sank when she saw the frosty glimmer in his eyes.
'I'm sure that you meant what you said, Adam, but I'm still
not sure that you'll settle down to the quieter pace of life in
Winton after what you've been used to.'

'Then all I can do is repeat what I told you. I have no
intention of shirking my responsibilities and no *desire* to do
so either.' His tone was harsh even though they had kept
their voices down so as not to disturb Hannah. 'Don't judge
me by what Claire told you, Beth. She made a mistake about
me and I hope that one day you will come to accept that.'

She wasn't sure what to say to that. Was she allowing
herself to be overly influenced by what her sister had said?
She hated to think that she was being unfair to him, but she
couldn't ignore the fact that Claire must have had grave
concerns about his ability to commit himself.

It was a relief when Hannah woke up at that point because
it gave her an excuse not to reply. She knew that she still
wasn't convinced that Adam had thought enough about his
decision to remain in England.

'Aunty Beth?'

She hurried to the bed when Hannah called her. 'I'm right here, poppet. How do you feel this morning?'

'I'm thirsty,' the little girl replied croakily.

'Then it's a good job that I've got a nice cool drink for you,' said a familiar falsetto.

Hannah's face lit up when Adam stepped forward, his handkerchief draped over his hand. 'Nursie!' she exclaimed in delight. She eagerly sipped some water from the drinking cup Adam was holding then giggled. 'Nursie hasn't got a mouth.'

'That's because she didn't have time to put on her make-up,' he explained with commendable aplomb. He turned to Beth and she was relieved when he smiled at her. It struck her just how much she hated to be at odds with him. She wanted to be his friend, not his enemy.

'Would you be so kind as to fetch my lipstick from Hannah's locker, Aunty Beth?' he asked in his shrill puppet voice.

'I'd be delighted,' she declared, then smiled at her niece. 'I won't be long, darling. I'll be as quick as I can.'

'It's OK, Aunty Beth. Adam's here,' the child assured her gravely.

Beth sighed as she left the room. It was obvious that Hannah had totally accepted Adam. Whilst a part of her said that it was a good thing, another part couldn't help worrying what might happen in the future. All she could do was try to protect her niece by not letting her get too attached to him.

She paused as a thought struck her.

Would it be possible to stop herself from making the same mistake, though?

It was almost midday by the time they left the hospital. Beth had been reluctant to leave even then but Adam had persuaded her that they should take a break while Hannah slept.

Now, as they stepped out into the bright sunshine, she gave a massive yawn.

'Oh, excuse me!'

'Ditto!' He covered his mouth with his hand. 'I'm absolutely shattered. I can't remember when I last felt this tired. I must be getting old.'

'You and me both.' Beth staggered to her car and rested her head wearily on the sun-warmed roof. 'I don't know if I've got the energy to drive all the way home when I'll need to come back here in a couple of hours' time.'

'Me, too. Or should it be neither?' He gave another massive yawn then shook his head. 'Brr! What I need is a large cup of coffee and something to eat to boost my blood-sugar levels.'

She opened one eyelid a crack and peered blearily at him. 'We could go to the hospital canteen or, if you don't fancy that, there's a café not far from here. I'll come with you if my legs will walk that far.'

'We can prop each other up.' He grinned as he offered her his arm. 'Four legs should be better than two, or at least that's the theory.'

'Depends on what state the legs are in,' she replied tartly, as they made their way to the gate. 'Mine feel as though they should be put out of their misery!'

'A cup of coffee and a BLT should do the trick,' he assured her. 'Can't you just taste it—all that lovely juicy bacon and tomato with crispy lettuce? Yum!'

Beth laughed. 'I'm so tired that I don't know if I'll be able to chew it!'

'You'll be fine once you smell the bacon frying. Trust me.'

He drew her arm through his and propelled her along the road. There was a lot of traffic about, considering it was Sunday, and they had to wait before they could cross to the other side. They turned down the street where the café was situated and Beth groaned when she saw that it was closed.

'I don't believe it! Of all the rotten luck.'

'Typical.' Adam looked along the road. 'It doesn't look as though there's anywhere else we can go either.'

'How about the park?' she suggested, rapidly trying to think of an alternative. 'There's a tea stall there and I think they sell sandwiches.'

'We'll give it a try,' he agreed immediately, turning round to head back the way they had come. It wasn't far to the park and Beth was delighted to discover that the tea stall was open and doing a roaring trade. A lot of people had decided to take advantage of the good weather and the park was crowded with families picnicking or playing ball games.

They bought coffee and sandwiches from the stall then found a quiet spot under a huge old oak tree and sat on the grass. Adam bit into his sandwich with relish.

'Delicious,' he mumbled through a mouthful of crumbly brown bread.

Beth contented herself with a nod because she was too busy devouring her own sandwich to speak. She wiped her hands on a paper napkin after she had swallowed the last mouthful and huffed out a sigh. 'That's better. I might just live!'

Adam laughed as he lay back on the grass and put his arms behind his head. 'Funny how you immediately feel better after you've had something to eat.'

She sank back onto her elbows and squinted up at the sky. 'You do, although I could do with a nap and *then* I would feel one hundred per cent like myself.'

'Then have one.' He rolled onto his side and she felt her heart flutter as he reached up and smoothed a strand of hair back from her cheek. 'It was a long night, Beth. It's no wonder that you're tired.'

'You're tired, too,' she murmured, praying that he couldn't hear how hard her heart was beating when she felt his fingers tracing a delicate pattern across her cheek.

He was so close now that she could see the tiny lines

fanned from the corners of his eyes, smell the warmly sensual scent of his skin—a mixture of soap from the shower
he had taken earlier and an aroma that was intrinsically his.
He hadn't had a chance to shave that day and his jaw was
shadowed with stubble, lending him a rakish air that was
very attractive.

Beth couldn't deny that her senses were stirred by his
nearness. She quickly averted her gaze because she was
afraid that he would notice. There was the funniest feeling
in the pit of her stomach, a sense of excitement and anticipation, so that she jumped nervously when she felt his fingers retracing the route they had taken. Her eyes flew to his
and she felt her breath catch when she saw the way he was
looking at her.

'I am tired and I don't mind admitting it. How about if
we both lie down and take a nap then neither of us needs
to feel as though we're letting the side down?' he suggested,
his deep voice grating so that the words seemed to take on
an added meaning.

Beth felt herself colour when an image of them lying together beneath the sheltering branches of the tree sprang to
mind. She didn't have to try hard to imagine how it would
feel to have him lying beside her, his body warm and hard
against hers...

'All right, then,' she said quickly, desperate to stop her
mind going any further. She lay back on the grass and closed
her eyes, and a moment later heard Adam roll over onto his
back. However, she was too keyed up to relax. She *could*
feel the warmth of his body all down the length of hers,
sense how hard it really was when he shifted slightly and
his thigh brushed hers, and her mind was suddenly awash
with images that had no right to be there!

'Relax. If you're worrying about Hannah, there's no need.
She's going to be fine, Beth.'

She almost jumped out of her skin when she glanced
round and realised that he was watching her. A flood of heat

swept through her when she saw him frown. 'That is what you are worrying about, isn't it?'

'I…um…yes,' she whispered, half expecting a thunderbolt to fall from the sky as a punishment for the lie. However, what happened instead was far more earth-shattering.

Adam slid his arm beneath her and drew her to him, nestling her head into the crook of his shoulder. 'Hannah will be fine,' he repeated, his deep voice rumbling beneath her ear. 'We won't let anything bad happen to her, Beth. Promise.'

He brushed a gentle kiss across her temple. 'Now, close your eyes and go to sleep. Everything will look much better after you've had a nap.'

He closed his eyes and after a few minutes the measured sound of his breathing told her that he had fallen asleep. She lay quite still, telling herself that she didn't want to disturb him by moving, yet she knew in her heart that it was another lie. She simply didn't want to have to leave the comfort and security of his arms.

She closed her eyes, feeling the heavy thud of his heart beneath her breast, the warmth and strength of his body pressed against hers. It felt exactly how she had imagined it would, and so right and natural that the tension seeped out of her. With a small sigh of contentment she fell fast asleep.

The patter of raindrops on the overhead canopy of leaves woke her. For a moment Beth couldn't think where she was before everything came rushing back. She turned her head and jumped when she found herself staring straight into Adam's eyes. They were so deep and blue that she had the craziest feeling that she was in danger of drowning in them…

'I was just debating how to wake you.' His smile was so warm that she felt a ripple of heat run along her nerves like bushfire spreading through tinder-dry forest. She had to wet her lips with the tip of her tongue before she could speak.

'H-how to wake me?'

'Uh-huh. I mean there's whole tomes been written on the subject, although I believe there's one tried and tested method that's particularly effective, or at least it seems to work for princes.'

His laughter was deep and strangely seductive. Beth felt another frisson of heat follow in the wake of the first. Maybe Adam was *just* teasing but it didn't feel like just anything to her. Was it any wonder that she couldn't seem to follow what he was saying?

'Princes?'

'That's right. Surely you used to read fairy stories when you were a little girl?' His smile was tender and teasing at the same time. 'Once upon a time there was a handsome prince who happened to be riding through the woods one day when he came upon a beautiful young woman who was fast asleep…'

'Oh!' She gasped as she realised what he had meant then felt her heart start to bounce around her ribs when he chuckled.

'Aha, I can tell you've remembered how the rest of the story goes. I've always wondered if any man's kiss would have woken Sleeping Beauty or if it really *did* take a prince to rouse her from her slumbers.'

The words seemed to hang in the air for a moment. Beth felt her toes curl in delicious anticipation. Was Adam going to kiss her? she wondered breathlessly.

It came as a huge letdown when he suddenly sighed. 'And now I'm not going to have the chance to prove it one way or the other because you're wide awake.' He gave her a last smile then stood up and stared across the park. 'Looks like we're going to get wet, I'm afraid.'

Beth struggled to her feet, thinking that getting wet was the least of her worries. Maybe Adam had been only teasing her but she didn't enjoy having her hopes raised then dashed like that!

'Looks like it,' she agreed stiffly.

'Maybe we should wait here a bit longer in the hope that the rain will stop,' he suggested, glancing at her.

She averted her eyes, afraid of what he might see on her face at that moment. 'It could get worse and we need to get back to Hannah.'

'You're right.' He gave a heavy sigh. 'Reality has to take precedence over dreams every time, I suppose.'

'What do you mean?' she asked curiously.

'Nothing. Take no notice of me.' He stepped from beneath the shelter of the tree and grimaced. 'Typical British weather. And to think that I used to lie awake at night, longing for a lovely English rain shower!'

She laughed huskily, wishing that she knew what he had meant by that strange comment. What sort of dreams did Adam have? she wondered. 'That will teach you. What's that saying about not wishing for something because you just might get it?'

'Meaning that nothing is ever as good as you think it will be?' He shrugged as he led the way towards the path. The park was clearing rapidly as families hurried to find shelter, and they were almost the last to leave. 'It depends on what you wish for, I expect.'

'So what would you wish for?' she asked, hurrying to keep up with him.

'That's simple. To get out of this rain.' He caught hold of her hand. 'Come on. Let's make a run for it before we get soaked.'

Beth let herself be urged into a run but she knew that Adam had deliberately chosen not to answer her question truthfully. Maybe he found it too difficult to admit what his dearest wish was if it involved Claire?

Her heart sank at the thought. She couldn't bear to think

of him spending the rest of his life grieving for her sister. She frowned as an even more unpalatable thought struck her. Even if he did marry, could the woman he chose ever be more than second-best?

CHAPTER NINE

BETH WAS exhausted when Monday morning came around. She had spent the whole of Sunday at the hospital with Hannah and hadn't left there until late in the evening. Adam had stayed as well, only leaving her briefly to visit his uncle in the coronary care unit. The good news was that Hannah seemed to be responding to the antibiotics and everyone was hopeful that the crisis was over.

She dragged herself out of bed when the alarm went off and took a shower then set to and ironed her clean uniform dress. Sunday was the day when she normally caught up with her housework and she groaned when she thought about all the jobs that still needed doing.

She snatched a cup of instant coffee then hurried down to the surgery. Eileen was in the office, going through the day's post, and she greeted her with a cheery smile.

'Was it a bit of a rush to get ready this morning, then?' she asked, tucking the label back inside the collar of Beth's dress.

'Thanks. And, yes, it was a rush. We were at the hospital with Hannah all day yesterday so I didn't have time to do any of my usual jobs,' she explained. 'I had to start ironing when I got up this morning.'

'What a shame! When you say *we* do you mean that you had a friend with you?' the receptionist asked curiously.

'That's right.' Beth turned away, making a great show of checking the diary so that she didn't need to look at the other woman. Until she knew what Adam intended to tell people about Hannah, it didn't seem right to mention that he'd been at the hospital with her. 'Looks like a full list this morning so I'd better go and get ready.'

She quickly left the office before the receptionist could ask her anything else and ran slap-bang into Adam, who had just arrived.

'Sorry! I should look where I'm going,' she apologised.

'Don't worry. I'm tougher than I look!' He gave her a warm smile, although she couldn't help noticing how tired he looked as well.

'You look how I feel,' she observed, walking along the corridor with him.

'I expect I do,' he agreed ruefully. 'It was a long day yesterday. It's no wonder that we're both worn out this morning.'

'But at least Hannah appears to be improving. I phoned the hospital as soon as I got up and they said that she'd had a comfortable night.'

'I know. I phoned them as well.' He opened the door to his room then paused, and she couldn't help noticing the frown he gave.

'What is it? I can tell that something is worrying you,' she asked quickly.

'I was just wondering how you're going to cope when Hannah is well enough to leave hospital. She's going to need a lot of care in the first few months, Beth. I don't know how you are going to fit in looking after her as well as doing a full-time job.'

'I'll manage,' she assured him, although she had to confess that it was something she had worried about many times. Hannah would be unable to return to school for some time after she was discharged from hospital because of the risk of infection. She would also need to continue her treatment, which would mean repeated trips to the hospital. It was going to be difficult to fit everything in when she was working.

'It isn't going to be easy,' he said flatly. 'I think we need to start making provision for when she comes home, see if we can work out a plan that will make life easier for you as

well as for Hannah. Obviously, I'll do everything I can to
help, but we have to face the fact that she's going to need
a lot of care in the first few months.'

'Maybe I could find someone to sit with her while I'm at
work,' Beth suggested, thinking worriedly about how much
it would cost to hire anyone reliable.

'Do you think that's a good idea?' He shrugged when she
looked at him. 'You told me that Hannah is shy with strangers. The fact that she's been so ill might simply exacerbate
the problem.'

'What else do you suggest? I can't afford to give up my
job to look after her because then we would have no money,
not to mention anywhere to live.'

'I'm not sure what the answer is but I do think that we
need to consider all our options.' He touched her lightly on
the arm. 'Just remember that we're in this together, Beth.
It's our problem, not just yours.'

He gave her a quick smile then went into his room. Beth
sighed as she went to get ready for her first patient. Adam
had meant to be helpful but it had brought it home to her
how much their lives were going to revolve around Hannah
in the future. Whilst she wanted nothing more than to look
after her niece, would Adam come to resent the restrictions
that caring for a sick child would impose on him?

It was impossible to answer that question. She would just
have to wait and see what happened. But suddenly it felt as
though her whole life was hanging in the balance.

Beth had a long list of appointments that day so she didn't
get a moment to herself. However, she was glad that she
didn't have time to think about her own problems.

One of her first patients was Hilary Dwyer, the daughter
of the woman who had been suffering from Wernicke-
Korsakoff syndrome. Beth had difficulty hiding her surprise
when Hilary came into the room. Not only had Hilary's hair
been cut and styled but she had bought herself some fash-
ionable new clothes. The transformation was amazing.

'You look wonderful,' she declared truthfully as she ushered the woman inside.

Hilary blushed. 'Thank you. I've rather let myself go in
the last few years, I'm afraid. I was too busy looking after
Mother to worry about myself. However, I'm hoping to find
a job so I thought it was time I did something with myself.'

'How is your mother?' Beth asked, getting out the sphygmomanometer. Hilary was due to have her blood pressure
checked, as well as having blood and cholesterol tests that
day.

'An awful lot better. Dr Knight suggested this wonderful
nursing home for her. I was reluctant at first but he insisted
that it would be the best thing for Mother if she had professional nursing care after she came out of hospital, and he
was right.'

There was a touch of hero worship in Hilary's voice.
'He's been absolutely marvellous. Did you know that he
visited Mother in hospital *and* found the time to call me at
home to reassure me that I was doing the right thing by
having her admitted to the nursing home?'

'No, I didn't know that,' Beth admitted with a smile, wondering where on earth Adam had found the time to do all
those things.

'I'm not surprised.' Hilary laughed softly. 'He isn't the
sort of man who goes around blowing his own trumpet, is
he? I feel so fortunate that he happened to be here when
Mother was taken ill otherwise we might have gone on the
way we were for years!'

'I'm really pleased that everything has turned out so well,'
Beth said sincerely. 'Now, I believe that you're due for various tests this morning so I'll start with your blood pressure
if you could slip off your jacket.'

Hilary quickly did as she was asked. 'This is all Dr
Knight's doing as well. He asked me to come in for a check-
up because he thought that I was probably run-down.'

Beth made a note of the reading on Hilary's card then

unwound the cuff. 'I see that you're due for a cholesterol test and a blood test as well.'

'That's right.' Hilary sighed. 'I've been getting dreadful hot flushes so Dr Knight suggested that I should think about HRT.'

'Hormone replacement therapy is marvellous,' she assured her patient, breaking open a new syringe to take the first sample of blood. 'Many women find that it makes a huge difference to their lives.'

'The only thing that puts me off is the thought of having to take lots of tablets,' Hilary confessed with a grimace. 'I hate taking pills.'

'You don't have to take tablets for the oestrogen part of the treatment. You can opt for an adhesive patch or an implant, if you prefer,' Beth explained, deftly drawing up blood into the syringe. She broke off the needle and filled in the label with the patient's details then picked up another syringe. 'However, the progestogen is administered in tablet form, I'm afraid.'

'Oh, I see. Well, I'm sure I can cope with one lot of tablets,' Hilary said, sounding relieved. 'Especially if the results are as good as you say they are.'

'I've had women tell me that HRT has literally changed their lives,' Beth assured her. 'As well as controlling the hot flushes and night sweats, which are so distressing, it helps to prevent osteoporosis—or thinning of the bones—and atherosclerosis, which is narrowing of the arteries. Plus, it does prevent dryness of the vagina which can make sexual intercourse very painful after the menopause.'

Hilary blushed. 'That isn't something I need to worry about. I'm afraid that if Mr Right is out there, I certainly haven't come across him yet!'

'There's still time,' Beth said, laughing as she pressed a dressing over the small puncture mark in the crook of Hilary's arm. 'That's it, then. We should get the results of the blood tests in a few days' time so make an appointment to see Dr Knight on your way out.'

'I shall. Thank you.' Hilary slipped on her jacket and smiled mischievously at Beth. 'Now there's a man who would come top of my list for the title of Mr Right. Lucky you, getting to work with Dr Knight every day!'

Beth murmured some appropriate reply but she couldn't help sighing after she had seen Hilary out. Adam would come top of many women's lists, she would imagine, but would he be at all interested to know that?

The rest of the day flew past. There was a baby clinic that afternoon, which Adam had offered to take instead of Chris. Beth got everything set up before she went for her lunch, knowing that she wouldn't have time after she got back from the hospital. Adam had a patient with him so she decided that it was pointless waiting to see if he wanted to go with her. She was always pushed for time because it was a good twenty-minute drive to the hospital.

She spent a quarter of an hour with Hannah then drove back to Winton, cursing roundly when she found herself stuck in a traffic jam. The Willows hotel had been extended recently and workmen were digging up the road outside. It was obviously a rush job because there was a huge banner in front of the place, announcing that the new bar and restaurant would be opening that evening. By the time she managed to get through the hold-up she was fifteen minutes late arriving at the surgery.

Adam had just shown the first patient into his room, and he looked up when Beth appeared. 'Can you find me Laura Watson's notes, please? They don't appear to be amongst the ones Eileen has left for me.'

Although his tone was pleasant enough, she couldn't help noticing the rather grim set to his mouth when he addressed her. Her heart sank because it was obvious that he wasn't pleased about her being late.

'Of course,' she replied, deeming it better to leave her apology for later rather than waste any more time. She hurriedly found the baby's notes and took them back to him.

'Thanks.' Adam skimmed through the child's record then turned to her mother. 'I see from this that Laura was born six weeks premature, Mrs Watson.'

'That's right, Doctor,' the young mother agreed. 'The hospital kept her in the intensive care unit for over a month because she had trouble breathing.'

'That's a fairly common complication with prem babies,' Adam assured her. 'How has she been since you brought her home?'

'Fine. She takes her feeds without any trouble now and she seems to be gaining weight at a rate of knots!'

He laughed as he lifted the baby from her mother's knee and gently deposited her in the scales. 'She certainly looks well. Let's see how much weight she's gained since the last time you brought her into the clinic.'

He quickly adjusted the scales then smiled. 'Six ounces. Not bad going, I'd say.'

Beth quickly noted the baby's weight and the date on her chart while he handed Laura back to her proud mother.

'You're obviously doing a great job with Laura, Mrs Watson. I know she had a bit of a setback when she was born, but she'll soon catch up. Most prem babies make up any ground they lost within the first year,' he told her in his usual calmly reassuring manner. 'Next time you come to the clinic we'll start Laura off on her immunisation programme.'

'That's something I wanted to ask you about,' Julia Watson said worriedly as she began slipping the baby back into her clothes. 'I've heard so many conflicting views about those injections that I don't know what to believe, quite honestly.'

'The risks of vaccination are far less than the risks of damage from disease,' he replied evenly. 'Obviously, it's a decision only you and your husband can make at the end of the day, but I do believe that it's important to have a child immunised.'

'But is there any point in having it done?' Julia Watson persisted. 'I mean, nowadays there are all sorts of antibiotics to treat these diseases with, so what point is there in having a child vaccinated against them?'

'Because the antibiotics available to us don't always work. If, for instance, whooping cough is recognised early enough then erythromycin can be given and can shorten the period of illness,' he explained patiently. 'However, it doesn't actually *cure* the whooping cough. I've seen babies die of the disease because they developed complications such as pneumonia.'

'Oh, I hadn't realised that!' Julia Watson shuddered. 'You tend to get a bit complacent, don't you? Expect that there's a cure for everything, but that's not always the case.'

'No, it isn't, I'm afraid,' he said flatly.

Beth knew immediately that he was thinking about Hannah. Even if Hannah had a bone-marrow transplant, there were no guarantees that she would be cured.

She longed to say something to him, a few words of re-assurance, but there was no time as he set about explaining the vaccination programme to Laura's mother. Each baby was given a combined injection against diphtheria, tetanus and whooping cough at two, three and four months of age. Another injection was also given to immunise the child against *Haemophilus influenzae* B, the bacterium responsible for epiglottitis and meningitis. The vaccine to safeguard against polio was administered orally at the same time.

'I know that you must be worried about making the right decision for Laura, Mrs Watson, but I strongly advise you to have her vaccinated.' He turned to Beth. 'Do we have any leaflets on the vaccination programme, do you know? It's always helpful to have something to refer to.'

'There's some in this folder.' Beth found one of the in-formation leaflets and handed it to Julia.

Adam smiled approvingly. 'Good. I should have known that you'd have everything to hand.'

She smiled back at him, relieved that he seemed to have forgiven her for being late back from lunch. She quickly removed the paper sheet from the scales and popped a fresh one into place while he saw Julia out. Maybe it was foolish but it felt as though the day had grown that little bit brighter.

The baby clinic came to an end at last then it was time for evening surgery. Beth worked her way through her list, wondering when she was ever going to get to the end of it. When she left her room to fetch a batch of forms that she had run short of, she could see that the waiting room was packed. By the time they finished just before seven everyone was worn out.

'The days just seem to get busier,' Chris exclaimed, following her into the office with a stack of cards for filing. 'It's fast reaching the point where we won't be able to cope.'

'I agree.' Adam had come into the office behind them and had heard what Chris had said. 'As soon as Jonathan is well enough I intend to broach the idea of taking on another partner.'

'Do you think Dr Wright will agree?' Beth queried.

'I don't think he'll have any choice.' Adam shrugged. 'It's obvious that the surgery is drastically understaffed. We not only need another GP but we need closer links with the community nurses' department as well. A lot of the people you deal with in the surgery, Beth, should be seen at home by a community nurse.

'Then there's all the office work that has to be done. Eileen does a superb job but she needs help. We need another receptionist plus an office manager to deal with all the paperwork that's piling up.'

Chris whistled. 'You're talking about making some major changes around here. I'm all for it, frankly, but I don't know how Jonathan will feel. It took me long enough to persuade him to buy in an on-call service outside surgery hours.'

'I think Jonathan will have to bow to the inevitable. This practice cannot carry on functioning the way it has been, with people running themselves ragged trying to keep on top of all the work,' Adam stated bluntly.

'Amen to that,' Chris said immediately. 'By the way, have you had any luck finding a locum?'

'I've got someone coming tomorrow as it happens, a fellow by the name of Benedict Cole. I spoke to him on the phone this afternoon and I'm hopeful, shall I say.' He clapped Chris on the shoulder. 'It might be a bit premature but maybe you can think about packing those suitcases soon.'

Chris laughed. 'They're already packed! I've no idea where I'm going, mind, but that doesn't matter so long as I get away from here. The only thing that's keeping me going at the moment is the thought of this break!'

Adam laughed as Chris sketched them a wave and left. However, his expression was thoughtful when he turned to Beth. 'Let's hope this holiday does him good otherwise I get the impression that Chris might consider giving up medicine altogether.'

'Do you really think so? It would be such a shame if he did,' she said worriedly. 'Eileen told me when I first started working here how dedicated Chris is to his job.'

'Maybe he is, but there comes a point when everyone has to face the fact that they need more than just work in their lives.' He shrugged but she wasn't deaf to the rather hollow note in his voice all of a sudden. 'I think Chris has realised that, and it's all part of the problem.'

'I'm sure you're right,' she agreed softly, wondering if he was thinking about his own circumstances. Like Chris Andrews, Adam had dedicated his life to his work up till now, but had he come to realise that he needed more out of life, like a home and family and someone to love?

Maybe he had found the first two by coming back to Winton and finding Hannah, but would he ever find a woman he could love as much as Claire?

She sighed, realising how often that thought had plagued her of late. It was a bit like having a sore tooth—she kept prodding away at it instead of leaving it alone. But it was the reason why she found it so difficult to deal with that worried her most of all.

It hurt to know that Adam might still be in love with Claire, and it hurt more than anything had ever hurt before, including her break-up with Ian. On one hand she wished that she understood why it should cause her such pain, whilst on the other she knew that it would be a mistake to start looking for an answer. Some questions were best left alone!

Hannah was sitting up in bed when they arrived at the hospital that night. Adam had driven them both there, claiming that it was pointless going in separate cars, and it hadn't seemed worth arguing. Now, as she hurried into Hannah's room, Beth felt her spirits lift. Although Hannah still looked rather pale and heavy-eyed, she was obviously much better that evening.

She went straight to the bed and gave the child a hug. 'Hello, darling. How are you tonight? You look a lot better, I must say.'

'I don't feel sick now,' Hannah told her. Her face suddenly broke into a huge smile as Adam came into the room. The sister on duty that night had stopped him as they had been passing the office so Beth had gone on ahead.

'Adam! I thought you weren't coming,' Hannah exclaimed in delight.

'Wild horses couldn't have kept me away!' he declared with a smile. However, Beth could tell that something was troubling him and her heart turned over as she wondered what the sister had told him.

It was impossible to question him in front of Hannah, of

course, so she bided her time. They stayed with the child for almost an hour then left when it became obvious that she was getting tired. There were a lot of visitors leaving at the same time so Beth waited until they were out of the building before asking him what the sister had wanted to speak to him about.

'The results of the blood tests are back. Charles Guest left a message, asking me to make an appointment to see him as soon as possible.'

'Did the sister give you any indication whether it was good news?' she asked anxiously.

'No. You know what hospital etiquette is like. It's left to the consultant to break the news.' He grimaced. 'I keep wondering what's going to happen if I'm not a suitable donor for Hannah. After that scare she's just had, it's more imperative than ever that she gets this transplant.'

'It is,' Beth agreed. 'We'll just have to keep our fingers crossed, I suppose. When have you arranged to see Mr Guest?'

'Tomorrow afternoon at 2.30. I was hoping that you'd come with me.' He summoned a smile but she could tell how anxious he was. 'I could do with a bit of moral support, to be honest.'

'Of course I'll come. It's my free afternoon because I'm working this Saturday, so there's no problem about that.'

'And Chris has agreed to cover for me any time that I need to come to the hospital,' he informed her, unlocking the car door.

'You've told him about Hannah, then?' she asked as she slid into the seat.

'Yes. You don't mind, do you?' He turned to look at her as he got into the driver's side.

'Of course not. I was going to ask you if you intended to tell people about her, in fact.'

'*If* I was going to tell people? What do you mean by that?'

She shrugged, feeling a little uncomfortable when she

heard the edge in his voice. 'I wasn't sure what you intended to do. I mean, this situation has come right out of the blue, hasn't it? I wouldn't blame you if you didn't want people to know that you are Hannah's father.'

'I have no intention of hiding the fact, I can assure you.' He started the engine with a roar that hinted at his displeasure. 'It wasn't my decision to stay out of her life, if you recall.'

'I know that and I wasn't trying to imply that it was.' She sighed. 'Sorry. I didn't mean to upset you. I was just trying to be…well, discreet, I suppose. People are bound to be curious about what's happened and I just didn't want you to be put on the spot by having to answer a lot of awkward questions.'

His expression softened. 'And I'm sorry for snapping at you like that when you were only trying to help.' Reaching over, he took hold of her hand. 'Friends?'

She laughed when he treated her to a hang-dog look. 'Of course!'

'Good.' He let go of her hand as they came to a junction. 'I'd hate to think that we might fall out, Beth, when we both want the same thing.'

'Me, too. Hannah's welfare is our number-one priority and everything else has to take second place to that,' she agreed lightly.

He flicked her a smile. 'It does for now, anyway.'

She wasn't sure what he had meant by that but before she could ask him to explain he suddenly groaned.

'Hell's teeth! I was supposed to go to the airport yesterday to collect my luggage. I'd forgotten all about it!'

She laughed at his rueful expression. 'It's no wonder, bearing in mind the day we had.'

'I suppose not.' He frowned as he pulled out of the junction. 'I don't know when I'll get the chance to go now. It will probably be the weekend before I have any free time. I know I bought some clothes to tide me over but I really could do with some of the stuff in my cases.'

'Why not go tonight?' she suggested. 'I know it's late but there's bound to be someone at the airport who can help you. They have flights going out at all hours.'

'Brilliant idea! Why didn't I think of it? But would you mind if I went straight away? It seems pointless driving all the way back to Winton when we're halfway to the airport.'

He gave her a beguiling smile. 'And as an added induce-ment, I'll treat you to a drink when we get back, so you'll not only have a tour of the lost-property department to look forward to but the pleasure of my company for an extra hour.'

'Oh, how could I possibly refuse such a tempting offer?' she replied, trying to quell the sudden pounding of her heart. After all, it wasn't as if he'd asked her out on a *date*! she told herself sternly, but it didn't seem to help.

'Stick with me, kid, and I'll show you a good time,' he growled in his best gangster voice, making her laugh.

'I'll believe you, although thousands wouldn't!'

'Then it's a good job that I'm not interested in their opin-ions,' he stated in a tone that made a frisson ripple through her.

Beth took a deep breath as he turned the car onto the motorway slip-road but it did little to quell the feeling of excitement that was making her blood fizz like champagne. Maybe Adam hadn't meant anything by that comment but she didn't want to believe it. She wanted to believe that she was *special* to him.

The thought was enough to make those bubbles start pop-ping all over again!

'Thanks anyway… No, really. There's no need to worry. I'm sure they'll turn up eventually.'

Beth smothered her grin when Adam tried to edge away as the girl behind the enquiry desk broke into another bout of abject apologies. It appeared that his luggage had mysteriously disappeared once again and nobody knew where it had gone this time. As he came to join her, she couldn't contain her amusement any longer.

'Ever get the feeling that those cases are jinxed?'

'I most certainly do!' he declared, rolling his eyes. 'I can't believe they've gone missing again. The person I spoke to the other day swore that once they had them back here they would lock them away!'

'They could have been liberated,' she suggested, her tongue very firmly in her cheek. 'There's a lot of strange people about so who knows if someone didn't take pity on them?'

'That's it!' He stopped dead and stared at her, laughter making his blue eyes sparkle. 'The SLF have freed them from oppression.'

'The SLF?' she queried, giggling uncontrollably.

'The Suitcase Liberation Front, of course,' he explained with a completely straight face as he started walking again. 'You must have heard of them? They're responsible for a lot of luggage that goes missing from airports.'

Beth was laughing so hard now that her eyes were watering. 'I thought I was mad but you are far crazier than me! The SLF indeed.'

He grinned as he opened the door for her. They had parked in the multi-storey car park across the road from the terminal and they paused while a car drove past. 'You started it. I was completely sane until I met you.'

He held up his hand when she gasped in outrage. 'Truce! We're both as mad as each other, agreed?'

'Hmm, I'll have to think about that.' She led the way up the steep concrete steps to the third level where they had parked. Despite the fact that it was gone nine, there were a lot of people about and they had to stop to let an elderly couple manoeuvre two huge suitcases through the door.

'Obviously not a woman who makes any hasty decisions,'

he observed lightly. 'Anyway, how about that drink I promised you? I thought we could stop off at The Willows, if
that's all right with you? Eileen told me that it's the grand
opening of the new bar and restaurant tonight, so it might
be fun.'

'Sounds fine to me, although I hope they managed to get
everything finished in time. They had the road dug up when
I passed there at lunchtime,' she explained. 'That's why I
was late getting back. It had caused such a hold-up that it
took me ages to get through the town centre.'

'Oh, I see. We'll have a look and if they're open, we'll
go there. If not, we can find somewhere else.' Adam unlocked the car. 'It must be a rush getting to the hospital and
back in your lunch-hour, without getting stuck in traffic to
add to your woes.'

'It is rather hectic. But it's worth it because Hannah looks
forward to my visits so much.'

'I'm sure she does, but it can't be good for you to spend
all your time rushing around like that.'

'I'm fine, really. So long as Hannah is happy then that's
all that matters,' she assured him.

'And you don't regret having to give up so much of your
free time?' he persisted, turning onto the motorway as they
left the airport complex. 'A lot of people would feel very
resentful in your position.'

'Maybe they would but I don't.' She took a deep breath,
wondering where the conversation was leading. 'Are you
starting to find it all a bit of a strain, Adam?'

'Yes, but not in the way that you mean,' he replied evenly.
'The worst thing about this situation is the feeling of help-
lessness it gives you. I'm a doctor and I'm supposed to know
how to make people better. The fact that I can do so little
for Hannah is very hard to accept. I feel as though everything that I've done since med school has been a waste of
time.'

'That's not true! Think about all the people you've helped

over the years, and all the lives that you've saved.' She touched his arm, feeling her heart aching when she heard the regret in his voice. It didn't seem fair that he should be blaming himself for something he had no control over.

'I suppose you're right. It's just very difficult to find a balance when your own child is involved.' He sighed heavily. 'I never imagined it would be this hard.'

'Had you never thought about having a family?' she asked, suddenly curious to hear what he would say.

'Once upon a time I did, but that was a long time ago. It seemed wiser to put any ideas like that out of my head rather than run the risk of being disappointed again.'

Beth felt a chill run through her. Had Adam been referring to the disappointment he'd suffered when he'd split up with Claire? she wondered sickly. Had he discarded his dreams of having a family because he'd lost the woman he'd loved?

She removed her hand from his arm, terrified that he might guess how painful she found that thought. It was a relief when he changed the subject and started talking about the proposals he had made for the surgery. However, she decided that it might be better to cut short the evening when they arrived back at Winton. Being with Adam seemed to unleash feelings inside her which she found it very difficult to deal with, and it seemed silly to put herself through any more heartache that night.

'Would you mind if I skipped that drink after all?' she asked as they turned into the high street a short time later. 'I'm really tired and I could do with an early night, to be honest.'

'Are you sure? Maybe a drink would help you unwind.' He slowed the car as they reached the end of the drive leading to the hotel. It was obviously doing a roaring trade because the car park was packed.

Beth shook her head, not wanting to be tempted to change her mind. 'Thanks, but I really would prefer to go home.'

The words were barely out of her mouth when there was a massive explosion from the vicinity of the hotel.

'What was that?' she cried, scrambling out of the car. Adam had leapt out as well and he came rushing round the car as a second explosion followed in the wake of the first.

'Get down!' he ordered, thrusting her flat on the ground as debris started to rain down on them.

Beth's ears were ringing from the noise and she could barely breathe thanks to the cloud of dust that filled the air and the weight of Adam's body pressing her into the ground. He waited until the aftershocks had died away before he got up and helped her to her feet.

She gasped when she saw what had happened to the hotel. The newly built wing had been completely demolished, leaving a large section of the roof listing dangerously. People were streaming from the exits, scrambling over the piles of rubble and broken glass that littered the path.

'What on earth has happened?' she asked in dismay.

'It looks like a gas main might have blown up. Use the car phone to call the emergency services. We need ambulances and the fire brigade here as fast as possible.'

'Wait! Where are you going?' She caught hold of his sleeve as he started to move away.

'To see what I can do to help. Hurry up and make that call, Beth. We're going to need all the help we can get from the look of it.'

'You will be careful,' she whispered, her heart turning over at the thought of him putting himself in danger.

'Don't worry. I've too much to lose to take any stupid risks.'

He touched her gently on the cheek then he was gone, disappearing into the crowd that was flooding down the path. Beth put through a call to the emergency services, but even though she responded calmly to the questions they asked her, inside she was a jittery mass of nerves.

She was just starting to realise how much *she* had to lose if anything happened to Adam.

CHAPTER TEN

'WE NOW know that there are three people still not accounted for. Mrs Evelyn Thomas and her grandson, Michael, plus the owner of the hotel, Roger Hopkins. My men are doing a sweep of the building to try and locate them.'

Beth's heart sank as the officer in charge finished updating them. There was a crowd of emergency service personnel gathered in front of the hotel. Most of the injured had been taken to hospital now and the police had put up a cordon to stop any sightseers getting too close. Although there had been no more explosions the possibility hadn't been ruled out.

She and Adam had worked alongside the paramedics, tending the injured. There had been so many people hurt that the emergency services had gratefully accepted their offer of help. Injuries had ranged from fairly superficial cuts caused by flying glass to the loss of limbs.

Although several of the injured were in a very bad way there had been no actual fatalities, amazingly enough. Now she felt her heart ache as she thought about the three people who were still missing. The fact that she knew them personally made the situation seem all the more desperate.

'Are you all right?'

Adam put his arm around her shoulders and led her away from the crowd. The fire brigade had set up arc lamps around the site and his face looked waxen in the cold glare they gave off.

'I keep thinking about those poor people still inside the building,' she admitted, shivering uncontrollably.

He sighed as he pulled her closer. 'They'll find them,

Beth. Those men are professionals and they know what they're doing.'

'I know they'll find them eventually but will they still be alive? I saw Michael Thomas only the other day when his grandma brought him into the surgery. He's only four, Adam, and he's so tiny!'

'Hush! They'll find him,' he repeated. Tilting her face, he looked deep into her eyes. 'They'll get him out of there, Beth. Trust me.'

She felt her breath catch when she saw the tenderness in his eyes. The fact that he was worried about her in the midst of all this chaos touched her deeply. But before he could say anything else, the officer in charge came hurrying over to them.

'We've found them! The man's trapped in an office at the rear of the building and the woman and the child are in the toilets. We've got a couple of paramedics attending to the man, but we need someone to look at the old lady and the boy before we move them. Is there any chance you'd do it, Doc? We want to get them out of there as fast as we can. We can't afford to wait until one of the ambulances gets back here.'

'Of course,' Adam replied immediately, letting Beth go.

She hurried after him as the officer led the way, feeling her stomach churning as she realised how dangerous it was for him to go inside the hotel. Although a team of firemen were attempting to shore up the roof with metal props, they were having problems making it stable. She was very aware that the whole roof could cave in at any moment and couldn't bear to imagine what would happen to anyone inside the building if it did.

Adam wasted no time as he dragged on a protective jacket that one of the firemen handed him then accepted a hard hat with a nod of thanks. Beth's heart was in her mouth as she watched him following the fireman into the hotel. It wasn't easy, squeezing between the piles of masonry, and she held her breath when a section of wall swayed perilously as they edged past it. They disappeared from view and all she could do then was wait.

It seemed to take for ever before they reappeared. Adam conferred briefly with the officer in charge then hurried to a waiting ambulance. Beth ran over to see what was happening.

'They've almost got the grandmother out but the child is well and truly trapped. It's going to take a bit more time before they can free him.' He nodded his thanks as one of the ambulance crew handed him a bag of saline and a line. 'I need to get some fluid into Michael stat.'

'How badly injured is he?' she asked, hurrying to keep up with him as he strode back towards the hotel.

'I'm pretty sure that his right leg is fractured but it's difficult to get at him so I haven't been able to examine him properly,' he explained. 'It's obvious that he's in shock, though, and he desperately needs fluid.'

He broke off as a young woman came rushing towards them. 'Have you seen Michael yet? Is he all right?' she demanded.

'Yes, I've seen him and he's alive,' Adam told her gently.

'Oh, thank God!' she whispered hoarsely, the colour draining from her face. Beth hurriedly put her arm around her, feeling the shudders that racked her body as she led her across to the ambulance and sat her down.

'I should never have let Michael wander off like that.' The woman clutched Beth's hand. 'I was cross with him for telling his grandma about the party when it was supposed to be a surprise, you see. I told him off and the next thing I knew he had disappeared.

'Evelyn said that she would find him but she'd only been gone a few minutes when there was this terrible bang. We were sitting by the window and Robert, my husband, was hit by some of the glass when it shattered. He didn't want

to go to hospital but they insisted. We didn't realise at first
that Michael and Evelyn were still inside the building.'

'It must have been dreadful for you,' Beth said soothingly.
Out of the corner of her eye she saw Adam hurrying back
to the hotel and quickly clamped down on her own fear.

He would be all right, she told herself. He *had* to be all
right. She couldn't bear it if anything happened to him when
she loved him so much.

The thought flowed into her mind without any warning
and she gasped. She loved him! It made sense of so much
that had puzzled her of late.

She cleared her throat when she saw Michael's mother
looking beseechingly at her. 'It wasn't your fault that they
were trapped inside. It was just a dreadful accident. You
heard what Dr Knight said, that Michael is alive. I'm sure
that he will do everything he can for him.'

'I know he will. It's just that I'm so scared!'

The woman broke into a storm of weeping. Beth put her
arm around her, wishing there was more she could offer by
way of comfort. She understood how the poor woman felt
because she felt the same. The fear that something might
happen to Adam was almost too much to bear.

It was a long wait. Evelyn Thomas was brought out of
the building by stretcher some ten minutes later. She was
deeply unconscious and the firemen who had rescued her
rushed her straight to an ambulance.

Beth checked her watch for the umpteenth time as Roger
Hopkins was carried out not long afterwards. There was just
Adam, little Michael and one of the firemen left inside now,
and it was obvious that the rescue teams were growing increasingly concerned. Leaving Michael's distraught mother
in the care of the ambulance crew, she hurried over to the
officer in charge.

'Why is it taking so long?'

'The kid's trapped in one of the toilet stalls,' he explained
grimly. 'Unfortunately, the area he's in was one of the worst

affected by the blast. Most of the roof has fallen in and the rest could follow at any moment. We're having to work very carefully in case we bring the whole lot down on top of them.'

He broke off as a deafening roar suddenly filled the air. Beth gasped in horror as she watched another section of the roof falling in. She couldn't bear to think what might have happened to Adam if he had been underneath it.

Tears filled her eyes at the thought and she turned away then swung back round when a cheer suddenly erupted from the watching crowd. Her heart surged with relief when she saw two figures emerging from the building. One of them was holding the tiny figure of a child in his arms and she knew without the shadow of a doubt that it was Adam, even though he was so heavily caked in grime that he was virtually unrecognisable. There seemed to be wings on her feet as she raced across the path towards him.

'He's got a fractured right femur and possible fracture of the right arm,' he rapped out, handing the child to the paramedics. 'He was conscious for a short time, but he'll need a CT scan in case there's any head injury. He'll also need X-rays in case of internal damage.'

'You can leave it to us now, Doc. You've done your bit,' the paramedic told him with a grin.

'Thank you, thank you so much!' Michael's mother called as she scrambled on board the ambulance. It roared away with its lights flashing and only then did Adam turn and see Beth standing there.

'Are you all right?' she asked huskily.

'Just about. I wouldn't want to have to go through that again in a hurry, though,' he replied with an attempt at levity. The fireman who had been inside the building with him came over and they shook hands before he turned to her again. 'We've done our bit now, so let's get out of here.'

She simply nodded because she didn't trust herself to speak at that moment. The fact that he was there and unin-

jured was almost more than she could take in. She followed
him down the drive, feeling the tremors of reaction coursing
through her body. News of the explosion must have spread
because there were a number of reporters amongst the crowd
gathered in the road outside.

Adam shook his head when they rushed forward to question him. 'Sorry, I've nothing to say.'

Beth hurried on ahead and started the car while he extri-
cated himself from the press. She turned to him as he slid
into the passenger seat. 'You don't mind if I drive, do you?'

'No.' He groaned as he sank back in the seat. 'I don't
think I've got the strength even to change gear, to be honest.'

'No wonder,' she said quietly, struggling to keep the qua-
ver out of her voice.

He reached over and covered her hand where it rested on
the steering wheel. 'Michael should be all right, Beth. So
should his grandmother. You can stop worrying now.'

'I wasn't just thinking about *them*!' she exploded, suddenly angry at his obtuseness. 'You could have got yourself
killed in there tonight, Adam!'

'But I didn't,' he said softly, so softly that her eyes flew
to his face. 'Were you worried about me, Beth?'

'Of course I was!' she bit out, gripping the steering wheel
so hard that her fingers ached from the pressure.

'Why?'

'Why do you think?' she replied huskily, feeling a frisson
ripple along each taut nerve when she heard the smoky undercurrent in his voice. She stared straight ahead, refusing
to look at him because she knew it would be a mistake. If
she looked at him then he would know how scared she had
been, maybe put two and two together and work out why.

Was that what she wanted? Did she want him to know
that she loved him when she had no idea how he would feel
about the idea?

'Pull over.'

She jumped when he spoke and turned to glance uncertainly at him. 'Here?'

'Right here…please.'

It was the 'please' that did it, she realised as she drew the car to a halt and switched off the engine. One simple word that somehow seemed to be imbued with all sorts of things that made her tingle from head to toe, made her heart race and her blood heat, made—

The rest of the thought disappeared abruptly as Adam drew her to him and kissed her. His mouth was hungry as it closed over hers, demanding a response that she was only too eager to give him. He kissed her and she kissed him back without making any attempt to hide how she felt. She loved him, and even though she hadn't told him so in words she was telling him that through this kiss.

He lifted his head at last and his eyes seemed to burn with an inner fire as they rested on her. 'Do I need to apologise?' he asked, his voice grating harshly.

'No.' She met his gaze proudly, refusing to lie either to him or herself. 'I don't want an apology, Adam.'

He drew his thumb lightly over her mouth, letting it linger on the soft inner flesh of her lower lip as he stared into her eyes. 'Then what do you want?'

'You.'

Something that looked almost like relief crossed his face before he kissed her again just as hungrily yet with a tenderness that seemed to turn her bones to liquid. Neither of them said anything this time when he pulled back. There was no need. Everything had been said…

Maybe not everything, a small voice reminded her. She still had no idea how Adam really felt about her.

She chased away the thought, refusing to listen to the voice of reason when her heart was telling her everything that she wanted to hear. Adam wanted her and she…well, she loved him. What more needed to be said?

They drove back to the surgery in total silence. It wasn't

far but she was trembling by the time she drew up in the
car park. She led the way up to her flat and unlocked the
door, gasping when he slammed it shut behind them and
backed her up against the hard wood.

She wrapped her arms around his neck, loving the feel of
his hard body pressed against her softness. She could feel
his heart thundering against her breast and knew that he
could feel hers racing as well. When his mouth found hers
she gave a small moan of relief because it felt as though she
had been starving for the taste of him.

'I could stand here all night and kiss you,' he murmured,
his voice sounding so deep that she shivered when she felt
its velvety tones stroking along her nerves. 'But I need a
shower.'

He smiled as he ran a gentle finger over the smudge of
dirt he'd left on her cheek. 'And so will you soon if I don't
get out of these filthy clothes.'

She laughed huskily, struggling to drag herself back from
the abyss of passion. 'There's plenty of hot water.'

'Sounds like an offer I can't resist.' He bent and kissed
her slowly, deeply, then looked into her eyes. 'Want to join
me?'

Beth felt her breath catch as she realised what he was
really asking. 'Do you want me to?' she whispered, the
blood drumming in her head so that she felt dizzy.

He laughed softly as he drew her into his arms and held
her so that she could feel the urgent thrusting of his body.
'What do you think?'

She smiled into his eyes, wondering how it was possible
to love someone so much. 'That I'd better go and find us
some towels.'

She slid out of his arms and quickly found what they
needed then went back to the kitchen, but there was no sign
of him there. She tracked him down to the bathroom and
her heart seemed to beat itself to a standstill when she saw
him. He had shed his clothes and was standing under the

shower with his back to her. Water was cascading over his head, flattening his black hair against his skull, streaming down his body.

Beth simply stood in the doorway and stared. His body was hard and lean, the muscles flexing rhythmically as he scrubbed himself clean. His skin was darkly tanned all over apart from a paler band circling his narrow hips and buttocks.

Her eyes lingered helplessly on that strip of pale, smooth skin before she forced them to move on, following the long, straight line of his legs to his well-shaped feet. The room was filling with steam and it seemed to lend a dreamlike quality to the scene. Maybe that was why she didn't feel embarrassed about standing there, watching him. Or maybe it was because she loved him. Why should she feel ashamed because she enjoyed looking at the man she loved with all her heart?

He must have sensed that she was there because he suddenly turned. Instinctively, Beth's eyes swept over him once more while she took rapid stock of the thick black hair that covered his chest, the masculine trimness of his waist. Her gaze slid lower and she felt the blood rush to her face when she saw the effect her scrutiny was having on him.

He gave a throaty laugh but she heard the edge of uncertainty it held. 'Maybe I should have made it a cold shower. What do you think?'

She lifted her eyes to his face and smiled gently when she saw the hunger that blazed in his eyes and which he couldn't quite hide. 'That it would have been a dreadful waste.'

He gave a low groan as he stepped out of the shower and pulled her into his arms. Beth lifted her face for his kiss, uncaring that her clothes were getting soaked as she pressed herself against him. His mouth was hungry when it took hers, his lips burning hot beneath the cooling film of moisture, and she shuddered because the contrast was just so exquisite.

He grazed his mouth across hers one last time then slowly
reached for the top button on her blouse and unfastened it.
She gasped when she felt a cool, damp finger touch her hot
skin, but he didn't pause until every single button had been
undone. He grasped the front edges of her blouse and there
was a questioning look in his eyes as he stared at her.

'Are you sure this is what you want, sweetheart? It isn't
too late to stop if you're having second thoughts.'

Her heart overflowed when she heard the tender concern
in his voice. Even though she knew that he wanted her desperately, he would stop if she asked him to. It was so typical
of him to put her feelings before his, she thought with her
heart overflowing.

'I'm not having second thoughts.' She raised her head and
met his eyes proudly, almost defiantly, so that he would be
in no doubt about what she was saying. Deep down she
knew that she could be letting herself in for heartache but
she also knew that it was a risk that she was willing to take.
'I'm quite sure this is what I want, Adam.'

She pushed his hands away and slid the blouse off her
shoulders then reached behind her and unhooked her bra and
tossed it onto the floor. He didn't say a word as he stood
there with the water thundering down behind him. She had
a feeling that he found it impossible to speak and understood
why. Sometimes words weren't enough. Sometimes the best
way to communicate was through actions.

She heard him draw in his breath sharply when she undid
the snap on her jeans and pushed them down her slender
hips. She stepped out of them and kicked them aside. All
she had on now was a pair of silky panties and they were
soon dispensed with. She took a quick step forward then
gasped as her body made sudden, shocking contact with his.
His skin was warm and damp and hers stuck to it as she
pressed herself against him, breast to breast, hip to hip,
so that she felt the wave of shock and desire that raced
through him.

'Beth!'

Her name sounded hoarse as it exploded from his lips, almost anguished, but she knew that it was pleasure he felt, not pain. He swept her up into his arms, lifting her into the shower stall, and she shuddered when she felt the heat of the water raining down on her. However, it was nothing compared to the fire that ignited inside her when he kissed her.

Beth wrapped her arms around his neck and clung to him as passion swept them away. Each caress of his hands as they stroked her wet body seemed to make the fire inside her burn all the hotter. She kissed him back, her hands sliding over his wet skin, seeking out pleasure points then moving on to find more. She was amazed by her boldness as she matched each caress he gave her. She had never believed herself capable of giving as well as receiving so much pleasure, but, then, she had never known what real love felt like before.

Her heart filled with joy as she gave herself up to the passion they were creating together. She loved him so much and as soon as she could think in words and not just in actions she would tell him!

Bright morning sunshine was spilling into the room when Beth awoke. She lay quite still, simply enjoying the fact that Adam was lying beside her. She could feel the warmth of his body flowing into hers, smell the scent of his skin, almost taste his mouth on her lips. Her senses seemed to be awash with him and she loved the feeling. She wanted it to last for ever but would it? Could it?

The first tiny doubt crept in before she could stop it and she frowned. Last night she had been swept away by her love for Adam and the fact that he had wanted her. She hadn't paused to wonder why. Now it was less easy to dismiss the thought.

Why *had* he made love to her? Had he simply been carried away by the moment? Or—

'Are you awake?'

The softly voiced question startled her and she jumped. She turned to look at him, feeling herself melt when he smiled at her. Reaching out, he looped a silky strand of hair behind her ear.

'Has anyone ever told you how marvellous you look first thing of a morning?' he murmured as his lips traced the path his finger had taken.

Beth shivered when she felt his mouth trailing kisses across her cheek. 'N-o-o...'

His smile was smug, his blue eyes gleaming with laughter and a wealth of tenderness that made her skin prickle with heat. 'I can't believe that. You're just being modest,' he whispered as his lips finally reached her ear and circled it with tiny, sipping kisses.

'I've not had much experience of waking up with someone beside me. I've only ever slept with one other man,' she confessed huskily, shuddering when she felt the warmly delicate touch of his tongue painting delicate patterns on her skin. She felt him go tense all of a sudden and a small jolt of shock raced along her nerves, almost as though an alarm had gone off.

'You mean Patterson, I assume?' he said roughly.

'Yes. There was never anyone else...'

She tailed off because she really didn't want to discuss her relationship with Ian at that moment. No wonder she had always marvelled at why people made such a big thing of sex when that had been her only experience of it! Making love with Ian had been a duty rather than a pleasure, something to get over and done with as fast as possible. She certainly hadn't felt the way she had felt in Adam's arms last night.

The thought flowed into her mind so sweetly that she knew that she had to share it with him. She turned to him but he was no longer looking at her. He was staring at the ceiling and the expression on his face at that moment drove everything else from her head.

He looked so *lost*, she thought sickly. So completely and utterly bereft that her heart seemed to shrivel up inside her as she found herself wondering what he was thinking about. Was he doing what she had been doing, perhaps, comparing their love-making to past experiences, comparing her to Claire?

A huge pit of despair seemed to open beneath her. It took her all her time not to let him see how devastated she felt when he turned to look at her. Yet when she saw the emptiness in his eyes it simply reinforced her fears. Maybe last night he had wanted her but in the cold light of day he must have realised what a mistake he had made!

'I'll make some coffee,' she said numbly, tossing back the bedclothes and reaching for her robe. She dragged it on, ashamed now of her nakedness and what it represented. She had made love with Adam for the simple reason that she loved him more than life itself, but she should have stopped to consider how *he* really felt, she should have stopped and remembered Claire!

'Not for me, thanks. I need to get home and change before surgery.'

Adam's voice was flat as he tossed back the bedclothes and got out of bed. Beth averted her eyes as he dragged on his clothes, unable to bear to look at him and recall what had happened. She led the way from the bedroom and with each step her despair grew even greater. Adam didn't love her! He never would. What a fool she had been to let herself dream!

She stopped when they reached the kitchen, waiting until she had composed herself before she turned to him. Even then she wasn't prepared for the anguish she glimpsed in his eyes before his lids abruptly lowered.

'I don't want you beating yourself up about last night, Beth,' he said tonelessly. 'These things happen.'

'Do they?' She gave a shrill laugh, fighting back her tears. 'I'll have to take your word for that because I lack experience in these matters.'

She opened the door and stepped back, praying that he wouldn't say anything else because she didn't think that she could bear it. Maybe he was only trying to help but every word seemed to inflict yet another wound on her battered heart.

He swore under his breath as he looked at her averted face. 'We need to talk about this but we don't have the time at the moment.'

'There's nothing to talk about. We went to bed together, Adam. We aren't the first people to get carried away and do something we later regret and I don't suppose we'll be the last. Let's leave it at that.'

'If that's what you want.' He hesitated a moment longer then shrugged when she steadfastly refused to say anything more. 'Fine. So long as we both know where we stand. I'll see you later.'

Beth closed the door after he'd left and went straight back to the bedroom. She wrenched the sheets off the bed and bundled them into the washer. She wanted to remove all traces of Adam's presence from the flat as fast as she could because she couldn't bear to have any reminders of the night they had spent together.

She set the dials on the washing machine then went to take a shower, feeling her eyes well with tears when she walked into the bathroom and the memory of what had happened there hit her. She could recall in exquisite, painful detail how he had held her and loved her with a tenderness that she had thought must have meant something.

She might be able to cleanse the flat of any physical traces of him but she couldn't do the same with her own mind. The memories were going to haunt her day after day, week

after week. Was that what he'd had to contend with? Had
he been haunted all these years by the memory of her sister?

The thought was unbearably painful yet in an odd way
she knew that it would help her to cope. Now that she knew
how Adam must have suffered, she couldn't be angry with
him. If making love with her had given him just a few hours
of release from the pain then she didn't regret it.

She loved him too much to deny him that bit of comfort
even though it was going to cost her dearly.

CHAPTER ELEVEN

THE ACCIDENT at the Willows hotel had generated a lot of interest throughout the country. All the daily papers featured reports of the explosion, and the photograph of Adam carrying little Michael from the devastated building had been used on most of the front pages. Consequently, the phone in the surgery never stopped ringing with calls from the media and members of the public, eager to know more.

Chris proved himself surprisingly adept at dealing with the press when dozens of journalists descended on them. There were crews there from all the leading broadcasting stations as well, and it was Chris who went out to answer their questions. Adam had flatly refused to be interviewed and Beth knew that they would have found it difficult to cope if Chris hadn't stepped in.

By lunchtime the furore had started to die down, although a few die-hard reporters were camped in the car park. With all the commotion that had been going on Beth hadn't seen Adam all morning and she had to admit that she was relieved to have had a bit of breathing space. However, when he tapped on her door, she knew that it wasn't going to be easy to pretend that last night hadn't happened. All she could do was focus on her work and Hannah, and try not to think about anything else.

'Eileen said that you were free so I thought you might like to meet our new locum, Benedict Cole,' he said politely, ushering a younger man with sandy blond hair into the room. He turned to the other man. 'Beth has been with us for just over a month now so you can see what I meant about us being a fairly new team.'

'Hi, Beth. It's nice to meet you.' Benedict Cole smiled as

he stepped forward to shake her hand. He was as tall as Adam, with dark brown eyes and an engaging smile. Although he couldn't have been classed as handsome in the strict sense of the word, she suspected that a lot of women would find him very attractive.

'Welcome to Winton Surgery,' she replied, returning his smile and trying not to look at Adam. That was like trying to stop a river flowing or the sun from shining because her eyes were irresistibly drawn to him and she felt her heart ache when she saw the grim expression on his face. Was he still torturing himself about what had happened the night before? she wondered.

'Thank you,' Ben replied. His voice dropped to a conspiratorial whisper. 'So how are you enjoying working here? I always prefer a first-hand account from the workers rather than a glowing testimony from the boss. That way you get a better idea what you are letting yourself in for.'

She laughed huskily, very aware of Adam listening to every word. Would she have gone ahead and accepted this job if she'd known what *she* would be letting herself in for?

It was impossible to answer that question, of course, so she deliberately blocked it from her mind. 'I expect you do. Anyway, there's no need to worry because I'm sure that you'll enjoy working here. It's a very busy surgery but the people are great and that's what makes the job.'

'It is indeed. It sounds as though I've made the right decision, then,' Ben replied with a smile. 'Where did you work before, by the way?'

'St Jude's. I was a sister on the coronary care unit.'

'Really?' He looked impressed. 'That's a highly skilled job so what made you decide to change direction?'

'Oh, there were all sorts of reasons,' she replied evasively. Fortunately, Ben took the hint and didn't press her. However, she couldn't help noticing the frowning look Adam gave her as he ushered the younger doctor from the room to introduce him to Chris. He paused in the doorway and she found that she was steeling herself in readiness for what he might say.

'You haven't forgotten that I have an appointment with Charles Guest this afternoon, have you? Are you still coming with me?'

She inwardly shrank when she heard the lack of emotion in his voice because it was such a contrast to the warmth and tenderness that she had heard in it the night before. It was an effort to hide how hurt she felt but she couldn't bear to make a difficult situation even worse.

'No, I hadn't forgotten and, yes, I still want to come.'

His eyes flickered with something that looked almost like pain before he abruptly looked away. 'I've got some paperwork to finish which may take a bit of time. Ben says that he's willing to start next week if I can get all the formalities sorted out so I suggest that you go on ahead. I'll meet you outside Guest's office just before two-thirty.'

'Fine,' she agreed quietly. She sighed as he left the room without saying anything else. They had got through that if not unscathed then unharmed. All she had to do was focus on Hannah this afternoon and she would be able to cope.

Oh, yes? a voice jeered. She would forget that her heart was broken?

She reached for her bag, refusing to let herself sink into a pit of despair. She had known what she'd been doing last night even if the outcome hadn't been what she'd hoped for. She *would* learn to deal with this situation for the simple fact that she had no choice. Neither had Adam. He must be finding it every bit as difficult as she was. That thought made her feel even worse.

Beth was a bundle of nerves by the time Adam arrived at the hospital shortly before the allotted time for their appointment. So much hinged on what the consultant told them that day that she was finding it increasingly hard to keep control.

The fact that her emotions were already raw from what had happened the night before hadn't helped either.

He took one look at her ashen face as he sat down, and sighed. 'You look dreadful. Are you all right?'

'Of course,' she began, then realised that there was no point in lying. 'Not really. I keep wondering what's going to happen if it's bad news.'

'We shall cross that bridge if and when we get to it,' he said, taking hold of her hand and squeezing it. 'What did you think of Cole, by the way?'

'He seemed very nice,' she replied flatly, unable to summon up much enthusiasm. She withdrew her hand abruptly, knowing that she was within a hairsbreadth of breaking down. Maybe his concern was genuine but she couldn't bear to think that he would feel the same for anyone in similar circumstances.

She stiffened as the office door opened and a couple came out. The woman was sobbing into her handkerchief and the man's face was grey as he led her to the exit. It was obvious that they had just received bad news and her nervousness increased tenfold.

'He seemed very impressed with your qualifications,' Adam said, his voice grating ever so slightly. She shot him an uncertain look and realised at once that he was as keyed up as she was but that he was doing his best to calm her down.

She felt her heart overflow with love and smiled at him. 'Thank you.'

'What for?'

'For trying to make this easier than it is,' she said simply.

There was the oddest light in his eyes as he looked at her. 'I wish you didn't have to go through all this, Beth. I just want you to know how much I appreciate all the sacrifices you've made for Hannah.'

'Sacrifices?' she repeated, feeling her heart suddenly start thundering inside her. It was the way that Adam was looking at her, she realised giddily. As though he *really* cared about her being upset. Maybe it was silly to let her mind greedily snatch that thought and start weaving fantasies with it, but she couldn't help it.

'Giving up your job and everything else. I…I just want you to know how much it means to me that you were prepared to do all that for her.'

There was a raw note of pain in his voice that made her ache because she didn't fully understand its cause. She was on the point of asking him to explain only Charles Guest's secretary appeared just then and called them into the office.

Beth got up, grateful for the support of Adam's hand beneath her elbow as they entered the office. Between the stress of the coming meeting and everything else that had been happening of late, her nerves were in shreds.

'Thank you both for coming today.' Charles Guest was a very busy man and he wasted no time getting down to business after they had shaken hands. 'I'm delighted to tell you that the test results show that Dr Knight is a suitable donor for Hannah. Congratulations.'

Beth let out a gasp of relief, scarcely able to believe what she was hearing. She looked at Adam and saw him swallow. It was obvious from his expression how relieved he was, and her heart went out to him for all the worry he'd had.

'That's the best piece of news I've ever received,' he said sincerely, getting up to shake the consultant's hand again.

Charles Guest smiled understandingly. He was a distinguished-looking man in his mid-fifties with iron grey hair and kind eyes. 'I know how you must feel. I was delighted when I saw the results. As soon as Hannah is in remission we shall go ahead with the transplant. I am optimistic that the setback she's suffered won't have had any long-term effects. However, I want you both to understand that we aren't completely out of the woods yet. There still might be problems to face in the future.'

'What do you mean?' Beth asked quickly, her heart turning over.

'I'm not sure how much you know about bone-marrow transplants,' the consultant said quietly, looking at them. 'Obviously you two have a better idea of what is involved than most of the people I see, but it's still a highly specialised area. Although huge advances have been made in recent years, occasionally things can go wrong. I would be failing in my duty if I didn't make you aware of that.'

'You're talking about the possibility of rejection?' Adam said bluntly.

'That's right. It's something that can occur even with a perfectly matched transplant, which we don't have in this case,' the consultant agreed.

'I don't understand,' she put in quickly. 'You just told us that Adam is a suitable match for Hannah. Are you now saying that he isn't?'

'Not at all. I'm confident that we can successfully transplant bone marrow from Dr Knight to his daughter,' Charles Guest assured her. 'At one time it was believed that donor and recipient had to share an identical tissue type before engraftment could be undertaken but we now know that isn't the case.'

'The best match is between siblings, I believe,' Adam observed quietly.

'That's right. There's a twenty-five per cent chance of any brother or sister being a compatible donor.' The consultant sighed. 'Obviously we had to rule out that possibility in Hannah's case because she's an only child. However, recent advances mean that we can transplant marrow from a donor who only matches one HLA haplotype, and we have a much better match than that in this case.'

Beth frowned. 'So what you're saying is that Adam and Hannah aren't a perfect match but they're good enough?'

'That's right. Forgive me if it sounds as though I'm talking down to you but it's a very complex subject. Briefly, it all comes down to antigens—a group of proteins that are present within tissues and affect the body's immune system,' the consultant explained. 'The main group is known as the human leukocyte antigen system or HLA system for short. People inherit part of this system from their mother and part from their father. The main role of HLAs is to defend against infection and tumours, and they have a huge bearing on the outcome of any transplant. The closer the match, the less risk there is of the recipient's body rejecting it.'

'But surely you can do something to prevent Hannah's body rejecting the transplant?' she said quickly. 'It's something that's done for organ transplant patients.'

'Of course. Hannah will be given immunosuppressant drugs to help prevent rejection,' he assured her. 'And the success rate is excellent nowadays. But, as I explain to everyone, things can sometimes go wrong.'

'We understand that,' Adam assured him. 'So long as Hannah has a chance that's all we ask.'

Beth took a deep breath as the consultant wound up the interview. Maybe it had been silly to hope that he would promise that Hannah would make a full recovery but she realised that was what she had been praying for. Her head was whirling with everything she had learned when they left the office so that she was no longer sure if the news had been good, bad or simply indifferent!

Adam obviously sensed how confused she was feeling because he took hold of her arm and led her along the corridor to the coffee-shop. There were few people in there at that time of the day so he steered her to a table by the window and sat her down.

'Sit there and I'll get us both a coffee. I think we need one.'

Beth sat numbly, staring out of the window, while she thought about everything the consultant had told them, but she still hadn't decided how she felt about it when Adam came back with the coffee. He placed a cup on the table in front of her.

'Drink that up. It will do you good,' he ordered, pulling out a chair and sitting down opposite her.

She picked up the cup but her hand was shaking so much that she had to put it back down when coffee slopped onto the table. She heard Adam sigh and looked at him with swimming eyes, unable to contain her fear any longer.

'I couldn't bear it if anything happened to her now,' she whispered brokenly. 'Not after we've got this far—'

'Stop it!' He took hold of her hands and gave them a little shake. 'You heard what Guest said—that the transplant can go ahead.'

'Yes, I heard, but—'

'No buts, Beth. It's good news. I know there are no guarantees but the odds are definitely better than they were this time last month.'

She managed a watery smile. 'I suppose so. I'd almost given up all hope of ever finding you by then.'

'But here I am. And, according to what we've just heard, I am going to be able to help Hannah.'

She heard the catch in his voice and sighed. 'It means a lot to you, doesn't it? I don't just mean the fact that this transplant could save her life but that you are going to be the donor.'

'I can't tell you how much,' he admitted. He ran his thumb over the back of her hand and she shivered, but he didn't appear to notice. 'Maybe it sounds crazy to you, but I feel as though I've been given a second chance to make up for not having been here for Hannah when she needed me.'

'Claire was wrong not to tell you about her,' Beth admitted, unable to hold back the truth any longer. 'I tried to persuade her many times to try and get in touch with you again, but she was adamant that you must never be told.

She…well, she cared too much about ruining your life, I suppose.'

'I know that now.' His voice grated and her heart ached when she heard the regret it held. 'I admit that I was furious with her when I first found out, but I realise now that she did what she thought was best—for all of us.'

She abruptly withdrew her hands and stood up, unable to sit there and watch while he tortured himself with the thought of what might have been. Nobody could bring Claire back and she couldn't bear the idea that Adam would never be able to love anyone else as he had loved her sister.

'I think I'll go up and see Hannah now,' she told him when he looked at her with hollow eyes. 'I was too worked up before and I didn't want her worrying what was wrong.' She avoided his eyes because she simply couldn't bear to see the anguish they held. It felt as though her heart were being systematically torn to shreds but somehow she managed to hold onto her composure. 'Are you coming?'

'I want to visit my uncle first.' He took a deep breath, as though struggling to contain the painful memories. 'I haven't told him about Hannah yet but I think it's time I did so. It's also time that I told him that I intend to stay on in Winton.'

He looked at her and she felt a ripple run through her when she saw the searching light in his eyes. She had no idea what had caused it but it made her feel uncomfortable all of a sudden. She had the strangest feeling that he wanted her to say something but she had no idea what it was.

'I'll see you later, then,' she said, quickly turning away. She hurried to the lift and stepped inside when it arrived. She caught a glimpse of Adam as the doors shut, saw the lost expression on his face and felt the pain run deep inside her because there was nothing *she* could do to make him feel better. She loved him so much but it wouldn't mean anything to him even if she told him that. She wasn't Claire. She was the wrong sister!

Rose Johnson was just coming out of the office when Beth

arrived at the ward and she frowned when she saw her. 'You look as though you've lost a pound and found the proverbial penny. What's up?'

Beth summoned a smile but it wasn't easy to get a grip on her emotions. 'I was miles away, that's all,' she hedged.

'Oh, heck! You've been to see Mr Guest, haven't you?' Rose grimaced. 'Sister Clarke told me that you had an appointment with him this afternoon, but I'd forgotten for a moment. How did it go?'

'Adam is going to donate bone marrow to Hannah,' she replied rather flatly.

'Why, that's brilliant news!' Rose exclaimed in obvious delight then frowned again. 'So why the long face? You should be jumping for joy because it's what you've been praying for, isn't it?'

'Yes,' she whispered, turning away when she felt her eyes fill with tears.

'Come on. I've no idea what's wrong but you obviously need to get it all off your chest.' Rose propelled her into the office before she had time to protest and sat her down on a chair. 'Now, tell your Aunty Rose what's the matter.'

'Oh, it's just me being silly, I expect,' Beth replied evasively. 'Mr Guest warned us that there might be complications if the transplant doesn't take.'

'He was just erring on the side of caution, I expect,' Rose said soothingly. Her face suddenly clouded and she sighed. 'And I imagine he was thinking about one of the kids we had in here a few months ago. We've had to readmit him because he's suffered a relapse despite having had a transplant. I know Andy's parents were going to see Mr Guest this afternoon.'

Beth sighed as she thought about the couple she'd seen leaving the consultant's office. 'That's probably it. I suppose he wanted to make sure that we understood all the facts.'

'I'm sure that was it. Anyway, just because one child has suffered a relapse doesn't mean that Hannah will be so un-

lucky.' Rose paused then hurried on. 'Look, tell me to mind
my own business if you want to, but this isn't just about
Hannah, is it? Has this anything to do with Adam, by any
chance?'

'Why should you think that?' she countered immediately,
but Rose just laughed.

'Because I know you too well, Beth. I can tell that it isn't
just the thought of the transplant going wrong that's worrying you. So what's the problem? Have you fallen for
Adam—is that it?'

'Is it that obvious?' She gave her friend a wobbly smile
but the tears were welling into her eyes now. 'I love him,
Rose. I never meant it to happen—I'm still not sure how it
did—but I love him!'

'And is that such a dreadful thing? From what I've seen
of the guy, he's extremely *loveable*.' Rose ticked off her
fingers. 'One, he's handsome. Two, he's sexy. Three, he's
kind. Four, he's brave—I saw that photo in the paper, by
the way. Five, he's—'

'Still in love with Claire.' She saw the shock on Rose's
face and smiled wanly. 'He is.'

'Are you sure? I've seen the way he looks at you, Beth,
and he doesn't give the impression of a man who's carrying
a torch for another woman.'

Rose's voice was tinged with so much scepticism that
Beth's heart lifted like a bird taking flight before she forced
it back down to earth. 'I'm sure. I look a lot like my sister.
He's probably reminded of her every time he...he looks at
me.'

And maybe pretended that he was making love to her last
night, a small voice whispered insidiously.

The thought made the tears spill over and run down her
cheeks. Rose sighed in dismay. 'But I thought Claire told
you that they'd just had a fling and that it hadn't meant
anything,' she protested.

'She did. But maybe it didn't mean anything to her but it

meant a lot to Adam.' Beth found a tissue and quickly blew
her nose. 'It would help explain why he decided to stay
overseas all this time, plus he told me that he'd given up all
hope of having a family after he'd been let down. He…he
didn't mention Claire's name but it just seemed to fit.'

'Oh, poor you! I don't know what to say, really I don't.'
Rose gave her a quick hug then sighed ruefully. 'Why does
life have to be so bloody complicated?'

'Complicated is the word. I don't know whether I'm coming or going at the moment.' She managed a smile as she
dried her eyes. 'And to think that six months ago my life
was all mapped out. I might have been Mrs Ian Patterson if
none of this had happened…'

She'd been about to make a joke about the lucky escape
she'd had but she stopped when someone tapped on the open
door. She looked round and blushed when she saw Adam
standing outside. She was only grateful that he hadn't arrived a few moments earlier and heard what she'd told Rose!

'James was doing a ward round so I didn't stay long,' he
told her as she bid Rose a hasty goodbye. His voice was so
flat that she looked at him in surprise, but it was impossible
to guess what he was thinking as he led the way along the
corridor.

'Did you get a chance to tell your uncle about Hannah?'
she asked, struggling to match her tone to his.

'No. I'll do it later.'

He opened the door to Hannah's room and there was no
time to say anything else. Hannah was delighted to see them
and chatted away nineteen to the dozen. However, Beth
couldn't help noticing how quiet Adam was. Maybe he was
thinking about what the consultant had told them but she
couldn't shake off the feeling that he was upset about something.

She frowned as she tried to recall what she had been saying when he had knocked on the office door, something

about Ian if she remembered correctly. A little spear of pain lanced through her heart. It couldn't possibly have been that.

The next few days flew past. Media interest surrounding the explosions at the hotel gradually died down, although the incident had an unexpected repercussion when Chris was invited to appear on a daytime television programme to discuss the state of the NHS.

Eileen brought her portable television into work and they managed to snatch glimpses of the programme between dealing with patients. Everyone agreed that Chris had come over extremely well, sounding clear and confident as he had argued his point about the need for extra funding at grassroots level.

The other good news was that Roger Hopkins had been discharged from hospital and little Michael and his grandmother were making excellent progress. In fact, the only time that Beth could recall seeing Adam smile that week was when Diane Thomas and her husband came into the surgery to tell them the good news. Oh, he was as polite and courteous as ever with her as with everyone else, but the easy camaraderie they had shared had disappeared and she missed it dreadfully.

Benedict Cole started work the following Monday and soon settled in. By the middle of the week it felt as though he had been with them for ages. When Chris announced that he was going to take his long-overdue break, starting from that weekend, no one objected. Everything seemed to be working out surprisingly well, although Beth couldn't help wishing wistfully that her private life would mirror her professional one.

Chris invited them round to his house on the Friday evening to celebrate his forthcoming holiday. He had splashed out on a round-the-world plane ticket and was very excited about it. Beth really didn't want to go because it would mean spending time with Adam, but she simply couldn't think of an excuse to avoid it.

Adam's continued coolness towards her was a sure sign of how much he regretted having slept with her that night, and she found the thought unbearably painful. She tried to keep out of his way as much as possible, although inevitably she saw him at the hospital when they both visited Hannah. However, he didn't arrive until she was ready to leave on the Friday night and she couldn't help wondering if he had done it deliberately to avoid having to spend too much time with her.

'I'm sorry I'm so late, poppet,' he said, bending to kiss Hannah. The little girl had been moved back to the ward and she was looking a lot better than she had the previous week.

'I thought you weren't coming but Aunty Beth said that you would be here,' Hannah told him at once.

'I knew that you'd phone if you weren't able to make it,' Beth explained when he glanced at her.

'Thanks. I appreciate that,' he said softly, his voice sounding very deep.

She felt heat flow through her when he suddenly smiled, and turned away before he could see the effect it had had on her. She had to stop doing that, she told herself. She had to stop wishing for something that wasn't going to happen! But it was harder than it should have been to stop her mind racing off along a 'what if' scenario so that tears welled to her eyes as she bent to kiss Hannah.

'Your eyes have gone all sparkly, Aunty Beth,' the child said innocently. 'Are you sad?'

'No, of course not, darling.' She managed a wan smile for the child's benefit but she knew that Adam was watching her. 'I'll see you tomorrow. OK?'

'Uh-huh,' Hannah said, picking up the comic Adam had brought for her.

Beth turned to leave, feeling her heart contract on a spasm

of pure pain when she inadvertently found herself staring straight at him. There were lines etched on either side of his mouth and a dullness about his eyes that made her want to put her arms around him and hold him, promise him that she would take away his pain if he would let her, but how could she do that? Adam didn't love her, he never would. It all came down to that one simple fact. The thought was unbearably painful.

'Are you all right?' He caught her hand and drew her to a halt when she hurried away from the bed.

'I'm fine,' she assured him in a voice that sounded as brittle as glass. She snatched her hand away and he didn't try to detain her as she almost ran from the ward. She knew that he was watching her but she didn't look back because she couldn't bear to see him looking at her with concern. He might care about her but he most certainly didn't love her!

There was a crowd of people waiting for the lift so she used the stairs instead, wanting to get away before she made a complete fool of herself. She made up her mind that there was no way that she could face going to the party at Chris's and decided to phone him when she got home and make some excuse.

Her feet flew down the concrete steps and she was almost at the bottom when the doors leading to the coronary care unit opened and a man appeared. Her heart sank when she recognised Ian and realised that he had seen her.

'Fancy running into you again. It must be fate.' He smiled thinly at her, making no attempt to get out of her way as she tried to pass him on the tiny landing.

'I doubt it,' she replied testily. 'Excuse me. I'm in a hurry.'

'Things to do, people to see, places to go,' he taunted. 'What a busy life you lead, Beth, now that you've taken up with our local hero. I saw that article in the papers, by the way. Very impressive. It appears that your Dr Knight isn't quite the low-life I took him to be. Mind you, I'm surprised that you're his cup of tea. I wonder what he sees in a little home-body like you.'

'Get out of my way, Ian,' she said shortly, glaring at him, but he only laughed.

'Oh, dear, does the truth hurt? Come on, Beth, you know you're only kidding yourself if you think he fancies you.' His face broke into a malevolent smile. 'You're just a convenience, someone to look after his kid when he goes off on his travels again, which he will. Knight isn't going to hang around in the depths of leafy Cheshire once his duty is done.'

'H-how do you know about Hannah being his daughter?' she asked, white-faced with shock.

'How do you think?' Ian laughed contemptuously. 'Oh, dear, was it meant to be a secret and I've gone and let the cat out of the bag? Mind you, Knight didn't seem worried if anyone overheard what he was saying earlier. I think he was more concerned about how he could get you off his back, to be honest. Rather a silly thing to do, wasn't it, sweetie, falling for a guy who wants nothing to do with you? No wonder he can't wait to get out of the country again.'

Beth felt a wave of sickness rise up inside her. Had Adam really said that about her? She didn't want to believe it but surely even Ian wouldn't lie about a thing like that.

She lifted her head and stared at him. Her heart might be breaking but she wouldn't give him the satisfaction of knowing that. 'Maybe it was silly but it wasn't half as foolish as thinking that I could ever love a man like you. Adam is worth ten of you, Ian. You're not fit to lick his boots!'

She heard footsteps on the stairs behind her and pushed past him. She hurried out of the hospital and got into her car, aware that she was trembling. She made herself take several deep breaths before starting the engine, terrified that she would have an accident in her less-than-focused state of mind, and somehow made it safely back to the flat.

She walked up the steps to the door then sank down on the bench as her legs suddenly gave way. All she could think about was the fact that she had become an embarrassment to Adam, a burden he wanted rid of. She should have realised it sooner because he had been giving out hints by trying to avoid her.

She closed her eyes, too stricken with grief to cry. She would have to find another job because it would be impossible to remain at the surgery in the circumstances. Maybe she could apply for her old job? At least then she could remain in the area, which was vital if Hannah was to maintain contact with her father...for however long he decided to stay in Winton.

Her mind spun as she struggled to work out a plan that would cause the least distress to everyone concerned. The sun had slipped from the sky and dusk had settled in when she heard a car drawing up below. She peered down into the darkness and felt her heart come to a full stop when she recognised the tall figure walking towards the surgery. Adam! What was he doing here?

She shot to her feet, fumbling her keys from her bag so that she could unlock the door and go inside rather than face him. She couldn't bear to have to talk to him after what she had learned!

'Beth.'

He said her name softly yet in a way that made her instantly grow still. Beth felt the blood drain from her head and had to clutch the doorframe as a wave of faintness washed over her. She knew that he was standing right behind her because she could feel his warmth, but she couldn't turn to look at him, couldn't bear to see the rejection in his eyes.

Was that why he had come? To make sure that she understood that he had no use for her except as a *convenience*, as Ian had put it?

'Look at me, darling. Please. It's really important that we get this whole stupid mess cleared up.'

There was anguish in his deep voice now but it wasn't that which made her gasp. It was that one single word, a word she had never thought to hear him use when speaking to her.

Beth turned slowly, feeling the drumming beat of her heart shaking her whole body. His face was lit only by starlight and it looked eerily pale so that the lines on either side of his nose and mouth appeared deeper than ever. He looked as though he had been carved from stone as he stood there, staring at her, so that for a moment her heart quailed until she saw the fire that blazed in his eyes.

'Adam...'

She wasn't aware of saying his name so that the sound of it came as a shock. It seemed to hang in the air between them, redolent with so many emotions that she bit her lip. Could he tell from the way she had said his name how she felt? Could he hear the love that was contained in that single word?

She closed her eyes because she couldn't bear to look at him. It came as an even bigger shock, therefore, when she felt his hands fastening on her shoulders. Her eyes flew open again and she felt her pulse leap when he smiled at her with a wealth of tenderness in his eyes.

'We need to sort this mess out, don't we?' he said, his voice sounding gravely deep in the silence. 'But maybe this will help make sense of everything.'

He kissed her then and his mouth was warm and sweet and everything she had dreamed about. Her initial murmur of protest didn't get past her lips because they were suddenly too busy returning the kiss. The sound only emerged when he raised his head and that was because she didn't want the kiss to end.

'I have a question to ask you,' he said softly. 'However, before I do so, I want to tell you what I just told Patterson.'

She flinched at the mention of the name. 'I don't want to hear—' she began, but he stopped her in the most effective way possible. Frankly, she couldn't have recited the alphabet after he had finished kissing her, let alone strung two sensible words together!

'So that's what it takes to keep you quiet, is it? I must make a note of it.' His smile was teasing and she shivered when she saw the warmth it held. 'I said that I was going to tell you what I told him, *not* what he told you. They are two entirely different things.'

'Are they?' she whispered.

'Yes. I told him that I was crazy about you, that I was head over heels in love with you, in fact. And that, if my suspicions were correct after what I'd overheard you saying to him, the feeling might not be completely one-sided.'

She saw the uncertainty that shimmered in his eyes all of a sudden as he stared down at her stunned face. 'Is it, Beth? Am I completely out of my mind to think that you might care for me?'

CHAPTER TWELVE

'I... YOU... Oh, yes!'

'Yes? You mean that you don't feel the same about me?' Adam sounded as though he was in shock and she hastened to reassure him.

'No! I mean that I do feel the same. I love you, Adam—'

She didn't get any further as he swept her back into his arms and kissed her with a hungry urgency that left her breathless and trembling. The only consolation was that he seemed just as affected by it as she did.

He sank onto the bench and pulled her down onto his knees with a groan of mingled relief and joy. 'Thank heavens for that! I had a horrible feeling for a moment that I might have made a complete fool of myself.'

He pretended to glare at her. 'Next time anyone asks if you're in love with them, make sure you get your yeses and nos in the right places!'

'There isn't going to be a next time,' she said softly, pressing a kiss to the corner of his mouth. 'This is a one-off, never-to-be-repeated occasion. I have no intention of falling in love with anyone else, Adam Knight.'

'Promise?' The seriousness of his expression belied the lightness of his tone and she smiled at him with her heart in her eyes.

'Promise.'

He kissed her tenderly, holding her close so that she could feel the shudder of relief that rippled through him. 'You can't believe how good it is to hear that after the past couple of weeks. I had got it into my head that you were still in love with your ex-fiancé, you see,' he explained when she frowned.

173

'Why on earth did you think that?'

He smiled when he heard her bewilderment. 'Because I'm rotten at maths and adding two plus two gave me the wrong answer.' He brushed a kiss over her temple as he nestled her head onto his shoulder. 'I just added up what you said the morning after we spent that night together and it all seemed to fit.'

'What did I say?' she asked, letting her lips skim along his jaw because it was impossible to be that close to him and *not* kiss him.

'About him being the only man you had ever slept with.' He sighed but she heard the pain in his voice which he couldn't quite hide. 'He had to have been very special to you, Beth. You'd not been tempted to sleep with anyone until you met him and—'

'And nothing.' She silenced him with a kiss then drew back and framed his face between her hands so that she could look deep into his eyes. 'I thought I was in love with Ian but I was wrong. I had promised myself that I wouldn't sleep with anyone unless he was the right man, but I made a mistake. Whatever I felt for Ian wasn't love. I know that now because I know how I feel about you, and there's no comparison.'

'But that day when you were talking to Rose in the office, you said something about you might have been Mrs Ian Patterson by now if circumstances had been different.'

'And I was going to add something about what a lucky escape I'd had, only I didn't get the chance.'

He groaned as he hugged her to him. 'And I've been going through agonies, thinking that I had messed up your life and that you must hate me for it!'

'Hate you?' she exploded.

'Uh-huh. I mean, I did seduce you that night after the explosion. My only excuse is that I couldn't help myself… What? Why are you laughing?'

She wrapped her arms around his neck and grinned at

him, her green eyes full of teasing laughter. '*You* seduced *me*? I thought it was the other way round. I mean, you were just quietly having a shower and—'

'And, indeed!'

He kissed her again, long and hungrily, smiling with a very masculine triumph when he saw the effect he'd had. 'Don't get above yourself, young lady. If there's any seducing to be done around here, I'll do it!'

'Chauvinist! That attitude went out with the Ark,' she declared, deliberately trailing her fingers down his throat and inside the neck of his shirt. Her hand encountered thick, crisp hair and she hid her smile when she heard him groan under his breath.

'All right, I give in. We'll seduce each other. How does that sound?'

'Fair enough, although we could do with working out a rota,' she declared with a perfectly straight face as she let her hand drift on over the hard, warm muscles, loving the way they flickered and bunched beneath her touch.

'Whatever you want,' he said thickly, nuzzling her neck. 'Do we really have to dot all the t's and cross all the i's right now?'

'Shouldn't that be the other way round?' she teased. 'You can't dot a t...'

'Who said you can't?' He swept her into his arms, ignoring her gasp as he shouldered the door open then kicked it shut behind him. He kissed her long and lingeringly then looked into her passion-drugged eyes.

'You can do anything you want when you're in love—dot a t...'

'Or cross an i,' she finished for him.

'Exactly,' he murmured as he carried her into the bedroom and laid her down gently on the bed. 'I love you, Beth.'

'Do you? Are you sure, Adam?' She wasn't aware of the faint uncertainty that had crept into her voice but he obviously heard it.

'Yes, I'm sure.' He sat on the edge of the mattress. 'But if you have any doubts, I want you to tell me what they are so that we can clear them up.'

'You are certain that it's…well, it's me you love?' she said softly, knowing that she had to ask him.

'Of course!'

She sighed when she heard his surprise. 'I know that I look a lot like Claire,' she began, but he didn't let her finish.

There was sudden comprehension in his eyes as he bent and kissed her. 'And you're afraid that I was attracted to you because of the resemblance?'

He pulled her up into his arms when she nodded and he looked deep into her eyes. 'You're wrong, darling. I was very fond of Claire but I was never in love with her nor she with me. Surely she told you that?'

'She did,' Beth muttered, laying her head against his chest because she didn't want him to see that she still wasn't completely convinced. It wasn't that she thought he was lying to her but she had to be one hundred per cent certain that he understood his own feelings.

'But? Come on, I want you to tell me everything that's worrying you, Beth.'

He set her away from him so that she was forced to look at him, and she sighed. 'I just thought that perhaps she'd made a mistake and that you had been in love with her. It would explain why you have never married and why you'd given up your dream of having a family, and—'

'Whoa! Steady on.' He laughed deeply. 'What a very vivid imagination you have, my love. Let's start at the beginning and get this all sorted out once and for all. I was never in love with Claire. I liked her and I was very sad when I heard that she'd been killed. We got together almost by accident when she heard me speaking about Winton, as I told you.

'I'd just come out of a long-term relationship and so had she. It gave us a kind of bond. Maybe it was inevitable that

we should have an affair because we were both on the re-
bound, I think. However, we realised almost immediately
that we were making a mistake.'

'So when you spoke about having been let down you
weren't referring to Claire?' she asked in surprise.

'No. It was someone else entirely.'

'Who was she? You must have loved her a lot if the
relationship had such an effect on you,' she said wistfully.

'Her name was Jane and at the time I thought that my
world had ended when we broke up. She was a solicitor and
she had no intention of going globe-trotting, which was what
I intended doing.' Adam gave a sudden laugh. 'Actually,
that should have been a good indication that I wasn't quite
so crazy about her as I thought, because it never entered my
head to stay in England so that I could be with her!'

'But you said that you'd put off any hopes of having a
family because of the failure of that relationship,' she reminded him, trying to understand.

'I know I did. It's what I'd told myself for years. I think
it was easier than having to face the fact that, apart from my
work, there was so little else in my life.' He bent and kissed
Beth softly. 'I got over Jane a long time ago. I can barely
remember what she looked like, in fact.'

'So Claire was right about you two, then?' she said in
wonderment.

'She was. She was right about a lot of things, even about
her decision to put off telling me about Hannah,' he admitted. 'I would have married her if I'd known she was pregnant but it wouldn't have worked, and she knew that.'

'Oh, Adam, I don't know what to say! I've tortured myself with the thought that you were still in love with Claire.
I even wondered if you only made love to me because of
that.'

'What a mess. But everything is sorted out now, isn't it?
You do believe me when I say that I love you?' he pleaded.

'I do.'

'Mmm, remember that phrase. It could come in very handy soon.'

He didn't give her time to answer as he kissed her again. This time he didn't break off to ask questions or to answer them. It was another example of how actions could speak louder than words and say far more...

The sound of the telephone ringing roused them an hour or so later. Beth groaned as she reached for the receiver. 'Who can that be?'

She just managed to bite back her gasp of dismay when she realised that it was Chris, phoning to see where she had got to and asking if she knew where Adam was.

Adam grinned wickedly as he took the receiver from her. 'We'll be there very shortly. OK?'

Chris laughed. 'Don't rush on my account!'

It was obvious that Chris had a good idea what had been going on and Beth blushed furiously. Adam laughed as he pulled her back into his arms and dropped a kiss on the tip of her nose.

'Chris is old enough not to be shocked, darling, so don't worry about it. I think he'd probably guessed how I felt about you, anyway. I know Aunt Mary has had her suspicions, not that it's any wonder. First of all I told her that I would be staying in Winton then I told her that I would be leaving.'

'Leaving?' She sat bolt upright in shock.

'I knew that I wouldn't be able to stand it if you and Patterson got back together,' he explained with an ache in his voice. 'I didn't want to leave here but it seemed the lesser of two evils. I decided that I would try to find a job close by so that I could see Hannah on a regular basis and yet not have to come into contact with you daily.'

'Did you discuss any of this with your aunt?' Beth asked gently as the last bit of the puzzle slid into place. She sighed when he nodded. 'Ian must have overheard you and he twisted what you'd said to suit his own purposes. He told me that you saw me as a convenience, someone to care for Hannah when you went back to your old job, and that you couldn't possibly fancy a boring little home-body like me,' she explained when he looked puzzled.

'Did he indeed? I didn't hear the whole conversation you had with him.' He smiled grimly when she looked at him in surprise. 'I followed you out of the ward tonight because I was worried about you. I just caught the tail end of your conversation with that slime ball and that was enough. I don't feel the least bit guilty now for giving him a bloody nose.'

She gasped. 'You didn't?'

'I did.' Adam's smile was unapologetic. He trailed a finger along her collar-bone then let it slide lower until it came to rest on the curve of her breast. There was a gleam of mischief in his eyes as he looked at her, along with a whole lot of other things! 'Do you really want to spend any more time talking tonight?'

'That depends,' she said softly, sliding down to lie beside him and glorying in the feel of his hard body pressed against hers. It was obvious that *he* had far more exciting ideas than simply talking on his mind!

'Depends...on...what?' he murmured between kisses.

'On the alternative, of course. I'm open to suggestions.'

'Oh, I've got plenty of those!' he growled.

Beth laughed as he pulled her towards him, feeling her heart swell with happiness. 'Then what are we waiting for?'

She wound her arms around his neck and gave herself up to the passion that ignited spontaneously between them. They never did make it to the party that night because they were far too busy.

EPILOGUE

'I CAN'T believe that we're actually bringing her home at last!'

Beth took a deep breath but it was impossible to contain her excitement. Hannah was being discharged from hospital that day and she and Adam were going to collect her after morning surgery ended. They had decided that Beth should take three months' leave of absence to care for the little girl so a new practice nurse had been hired and would start work the following week. In fact, so much had happened in the past few months that sometimes she felt as though she should pinch herself in case she was dreaming!

The transplant had gone smoothly and the signs all pointed to the fact that it had been a success. Obviously, there was still a long way to go before Hannah could be declared free of the disease but even the ever-cautious Charles Guest had admitted to being pleased with her progress.

Beth had moved from the flat above the surgery and gone to live with Adam at his aunt's and uncle's old house. The older couple had decided to move to their cottage in Wales after Jonathan Wright had left hospital. Evidently, Jonathan had been putting off his retirement in the hope that Adam would one day take over the practice from him.

Now Jonathan and Mary were looking forward to spending some time together, and to having Hannah to stay with them when she was well enough. They adored their new little great-niece and Beth couldn't help thinking how wonderfully well everything had turned out for all of them.

'What's that smile for?' Adam asked, coming up behind her and putting his arms around her so that he could nuzzle her neck. They had been the first to arrive at the surgery that morning and Beth was making some coffee because they had *somehow* got sidetracked and missed having any breakfast!

She smiled at the delicious memory of their love-making and heard him laugh. 'I wonder if I can guess what you're thinking about?' he teased, letting his lips skim to her jaw so that he could leave a trail of kisses along it.

'I bet you can!' She turned to face him, loving the warmth and tenderness that she could see in his eyes. Every time that Adam looked at her, she could tell just how much he loved her, but it probably worked both ways. It was impossible to hide how much she adored him so she didn't bother trying!

'You were right, of course, but I was also thinking how well everything has worked out,' she told him, reaching up to return his kiss. She got sidetracked again for a few delicious seconds and had to think hard before she could recall what she'd been saying. 'Hannah didn't just find her father when she found you, she got a whole new family as well.'

'Maybe that family will grow in the not-too-distant future,' he said softly. 'I'm sure she would love to have a little brother or sister to play with. Once we set the date for the wedding maybe we could think about it.'

'I'd like that,' she whispered huskily. 'How many children should we have, do you think? I'd like two, a boy and a girl. That way Hannah will have a sister and a brother. '

'I don't care how many or what sex they are because I shall love them all,' he declared deeply. 'So now that's settled, when are you going to marry me? This week, next, the week after?'

She laughed. 'I think it might need a *little* longer than that to get everything arranged! Anyway, I want Hannah to be my bridesmaid and she won't be able to do that until Mr Guest gives us the all-clear.'

'That could take months! I don't think I can wait that

long.' He kissed her long and thoroughly. 'I want to know that you're mine for ever and always, darling.'

'You don't need a piece of paper to know that. I love you, Adam. I want to spend the rest of my life with you.' She paused but this was something she had thought about for some time and it needed to be said. 'It won't make any difference where you decide to work in the future either, because I shall always be with you.'

He swallowed hard and she heard the huskiness in his voice. 'Thank you for saying that. It means more than I can tell you. But I don't want to go anywhere. I've done everything I ever wanted to do, and now that I have you and Hannah to make my life complete, I don't need to go wandering the world. I want to stay right here in Winton and spend the rest of my days simply loving you.'

He kissed her again, only breaking off when there was a burst of exaggeratedly noisy coughing from the doorway. They both looked round rather dazedly and saw Ben Cole standing there.

'Sorry to interrupt but Chris is on the phone and he wants to speak to you, Adam,' he told them with a grin.

'Never even heard the phone ringing,' Adam replied, totally unruffled about them having been caught in an embrace. He dropped a last kiss on Beth's mouth then hurried from the room.

Ben chuckled softly as he picked up a mug and filled it with coffee. 'I wish I could bottle some of your happiness. It's a real tonic, working around you two!'

She laughed at that. She had grown very fond of the young locum since he'd been working at the surgery, and would be sorry to see him leave when Chris came back. 'So long as you aren't embarrassed.'

'No way! If more people shared their happiness, the world would be a better place. We hear too much doom and gloom all the time—it makes a refreshing change to see a couple who are obviously ecstatically happy with each other.'

'There's no one special in your life, then?' she asked, picking up the pot.

'No.' Ben heaved a sigh. 'If Miss Right is out there, I haven't found her yet, worse luck.'

Beth smiled sympathetically at him, although she couldn't help thinking that he wouldn't need to look very hard to find a woman to love him. Still, she understood what he meant about it having to be the right person, she thought as Adam came back into the staffroom. There was no point in simply settling for second best.

'Well, Chris certainly knows how to drop a bombshell,' he declared, accepting the cup of coffee that she had poured for him. 'He was phoning to tell me that he's been offered a job in New Zealand and that he's thinking seriously about accepting it.'

'Really?' She couldn't hide her surprise. 'It's going to create problems here if he does decide to stay over there, isn't it?'

Adam shrugged. 'Some, but we'll cope.' He turned to Ben. 'What would you say if I asked you to stay on here? We could make the job permanent, maybe think of it being a partnership if you liked the idea?'

'I'd say yes, please!' Ben looked delighted as he shook Adam's hand. 'I was dreading the thought of Chris coming back, to be honest, because I didn't want to have to leave here.'

'That settles it, then,' Adam declared. 'I'll phone Chris back and tell him that it's up to him if he wants to accept the job. There's no pressure on him to come back now that we have you on board permanently.'

He went to the door, pausing when Beth put down her cup and hurried after him. 'I'd like to speak to Chris and wish him good luck. I'm so pleased that he seems to have found what he wanted in life.'

'Amen to that,' he agreed, looping an arm around her shoulders. They went to the office and put through the call.

Adam hung up after a delighted Chris had thanked him profusely, and smiled at her. 'Another happy soul, from the sound of it.'

'Maybe some of our happiness is rubbing off,' she suggested softly, thinking back to what Ben had said.

'We have enough of it to share,' he said with a throb in his voice. He took hold of her hands. 'Have I told you how much I love you?'

'Oh, not since at least half an hour ago,' she declared with a mock frown. 'It's not good enough!'

'It certainly isn't. Half an hour is far too long.' He kissed her quickly then glanced at his watch.

'Making a note of when you need to tell me again?' she teased.

'I don't need any reminders,' he assured her. 'No, I was just working out that it's only three hours until we collect Hannah and bring her home with us.'

'Then we'll be a real family,' she said softly. 'You, me and—'

'Hannah,' he finished for her. 'I never thought that I'd be so lucky, Beth. I've found a daughter I never knew I had and one day soon I shall have you as my wife. I'm a very lucky man.'

'And I'm a very lucky woman,' she murmured as he kissed her.

'Lucky *and* loved,' he whispered. And she smiled because that was the most important thing of all, to be loved.

Modern Romance™
...seduction and
passion guaranteed

Tender Romance™
...love affairs that
last a lifetime

Sensual Romance™
...sassy, sexy and
seductive

Sizzling Romance™
...sultry days and
steamy nights

Medical Romance™
...medical drama on
the pulse

Historical Romance™
...rich, vivid and
passionate

29 new titles every month.

*With all kinds of Romance for
every kind of mood...*

MILLS & BOON®

Makes any time special™

MAT3

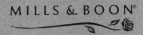

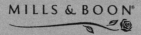

MILLS & BOON®

Medical Romance™

THE SURGEON'S SECRET by *Lucy Clark*

Part 2 of the McElroys trilogy

Dr Alex Page can't risk getting involved with beautiful
new research fellow Jordanne McElroy, despite the
fact she's everything he's ever wanted in a woman.
She is determined to break his resolve, and the closer
she gets to his heart, the closer she gets to the secret
he's convinced will drive her away.

MALE MIDWIFE by *Gill Sanderson*

Nursing manager Joy Taylor began to believe she had
a future with her unit's only male midwife — even
though Chris told her he could never give her a child.
But when a million-to-one chance changed everything,
instead of sealing their future, it threatened to tear
them apart...

STARRING DR KENNEDY by *Flora Sinclair*

When a tall hunk of a film star shadows Dr Skye
Kennedy around the hospital, she's worried about his
effect on the patients — and on *her!* Kyle Sullivan had
broken her heart before, so how would she ever be
able to trust him again?

On sale 5th October 2001

*Available at most branches of WH Smith, Tesco,
Martins, Borders, Easons, Sainsbury, Woolworth
and most good paperback bookshops* 0901/03b

Coming Home

Scandal drove David away
Now love will draw him home . . .

PENNY JORDAN

Published 21st September

FREE
4 BOOKS
AND A SURPRISE GIFT!

We would like to take this opportunity to thank you for reading this Mills & Boon® book by offering you the chance to take FOUR more specially selected titles from the Medical Romance™ series absolutely FREE! We're also making this offer to introduce you to the benefits of the Reader Service™ —

- ★ FREE home delivery
- ★ FREE monthly Newsletter
- ★ FREE gifts and competitions
- ★ Exclusive Reader Service discounts
- ★ Books available before they're in the shops

Accepting these FREE books and gift places you under no obligation to buy; you may cancel at any time, even after receiving your free shipment. Simply complete your details below and return the entire page to the address below. **_You don't even need a stamp!_**

YES! Please send me 4 free Medical Romance books and a surprise gift. I understand that unless you hear from me, I will receive 6 superb new titles every month for just £2.49 each, postage and packing free. I am under no obligation to purchase any books and may cancel my subscription at any time. The free books and gift will be mine to keep in any case.

MIZEC

Ms/Mrs/Miss/Mr ....Initials ....
BLOCK CAPITALS PLEASE

Surname ....

Address ....

....

....Postcode ....

Send this whole page to:
UK: FREEPOST CN81, Croydon, CR9 3WZ
EIRE: PO Box 4546, Kilcock, County Kildare (stamp required)

Offer valid in UK and Eire only and not available to current Reader Service subscribers to this series. We reserve the right to refuse an application and applicants must be aged 18 years or over. Only one application per household. Terms and prices subject to change without notice. Offer expires 31st December 2001. As a result of this application, you may receive offers from other carefully selected companies. If you would prefer not to share in this opportunity please write to The Data Manager at the address above.

Mills & Boon® is a registered trademark owned by Harlequin Mills & Boon Limited.
Medical Romance™ is being used as a trademark.